P9-DDW-026

RUTHLESS

RUTHLESS

CAROLYN LEE ADAMS

Simon Pulse

New York London Toronto Sydney New Delhi

This book is a work of fiction. Any references to historical events, real people, or real places are used fictitiously. Other names, characters, places, and events are products of the author's imagination, and any resemblance to actual events or places or persons, living or dead, is entirely coincidental.

SIMON PULSE
An imprint of Simon & Schuster Children's Publishing Division
1230 Avenue of the Americas, New York, NY 10020
First Simon Pulse hardcover edition July 2015

For information about special discounts for bulk purchases, please contact
Simon & Schuster Special Sales at 1-866-506-1949 or business@simonandschuster.com.
The Simon & Schuster Speakers Bureau can bring authors to your live event.
For more information or to book an event contact the Simon & Schuster Speakers Bureau
at 1-866-248-3049 or visit our website at www.simonspeakers.com.
Jacket designed by Karina Granda
Interior designed by Tom Daly
The text of this book was set in ITC New Baskerville Std.
Manufactured in the United States of America
2 4 6 8 10 9 7 5 3 1
Library of Congress Cataloging-in-Publication Data
Adams, Carolyn Lee.
Ruthless / Carolyn Lee Adams. — First Simon Pulse hardcover edition.
p. cm.
Summary: When Ruth is kidnapped, she's determined not to
become this serial killer's next trophy. After she's able to escape, her
captor begins stalking her through the wilderness.
[1. Kidnapping—Fiction. 2. Serial murderers—Fiction. 3. Survival—Fiction.
4. Conduct of life—Fiction.] I. Title.
PZ7.1.A23Rut 2015 [Fic]—dc23 2014022770
ISBN 978-1-4814-2262-8 (hc)
ISBN 978-1-4814-2264-2 (eBook)

To all the survivors out there—keep on fighting until you're thriving.

utter (adj) 彻地的.
courtesy (n) 礼貌. (adj) 出于礼节的.
awry (adj) 错误的.
hay (n) 干草.
ranch (n) 大农场.
tractor (n) 拖拉机.
gut (n) 内脏, 胆量.
Smother (vt) 使窒息. (vi) 窒息.

I CAN'T SEE. I DON'T KNOW WHY I CAN'T SEE.

I do know I was just dreaming. Running in a white dress through a field of wildflowers, no less. It was like a commercial for laundry detergent or tampons or a prescription medication that has death listed as a possible side effect. The dream is embarrassing, but it's better than the here and now. I try to crawl back into the dream, but it won't have me. Reality rushes in, faster and faster, chasing the dream away, replacing it with complete and utter darkness.

I need to open my eyes. I don't know anything else, but I know that. I try to open them.

Nothing happens. Just blackness.

Don't panic.

Think.

Thinking is hard and I know why. Concussion. My fourth one.

First two came courtesy of falling off horses. The third was the result of a PE flag-football game gone awry. I forgot about the flags, tackled a guy three times my size. His heel cracked against my forehead, but he didn't get the touchdown.

Focus.

Did I fall off Tucker? Somehow that seems wrong, seems impossible. I look for the memory, knowing it has to be around here somewhere. Tucker has an abscess in his right front hoof. He's on stall rest. Did I fall off another horse? That doesn't seem right either.

But it seems the most likely. So what next? And why can't I see?

Check if anything is broken.

I start with my toes. They wiggle. I can feel them. This is good. It seems they're inside boots, so maybe I did fall off a horse. My legs are oddly stiff, like they're too heavy to move. I try to bend a knee, but it isn't happening. My right arm is a no go. There's pain there. A lot of pain. It's dulled by the concussion, but that arm is a sleeping bear I don't want to prod. Luckily, I'm left-handed.

The left arm isn't hurt, but it also doesn't want to move. Not as bad as the legs, though, or the injured right arm. I think this left arm can get me somewhere.

Time to summon the will to move it.

Take a deep breath. . . .

Dirt falls into my mouth. Not dirt. Manure and shavings, something spiky. It's hay. Hay and shavings and manure.

I feel it now, pressing up against my neck and jaw, against my body and legs. It's dangerously close to my nose, and it's why I can't move. It's pressing down on me, pinning me in place.

Adrenaline hits my bloodstream. I fight my left arm free, dig the muck away from my mouth, and take a swallow of clean air.

Slow your breathing. Slow it down. Do it.

Nothing but air. It's all I think about for several minutes. I calm down, and the adrenaline ebbs away. I want to fall back to sleep. Sleep is soothing. Quiet. Peaceful. There's a field of wildflowers on the other side of sleep.

No.

I have to fight the concussion. I need to open my eyes. Maybe the dirt was pressed against my eyes. Maybe that's why I couldn't see. Hope gives me new energy. I try again, and get nowhere.

Maybe I don't have eyes anymore.

True fear now. For the first time. My thinking is clear enough for real, raw, primal fear to sink in. Time to be courageous. Time to check. But I don't want to know.

Be brave.

I take my left hand and reach for my eyes. There's something weird there, but I don't know what it is. It's almost rough. But there's definitely blood. Lots and lots of it. Sticky, heavy blood.

I jerk my hand away and strike metal. There's something metal above my face.

The fear broadens into something deeper. I am in trouble. Dear God, I am in trouble. I don't know what kind of trouble, but I know it's bad. Do my parents know? Am I alone?

I try to listen. Dirt muffles my hearing. My ears are halfway encased in the filth, but it seems like there isn't anything to hear. Except a hum. A deep, resonating hum that overwhelms everything.

Concussion. I know you well, old friend. Now kindly get the hell away from me. You may leave my hearing on your way out.

A wave of nausea crashes over me. I don't know where I am, but my best guess is somewhere on the ranch. Possibly under the manure pile. Was I in a tractor accident? Tractor chores are not my favorite. I lack skills, to put it mildly. But I won't let that damn tractor win, so I drag the arena, push the manure pile back, and do all the things the hired hands do.

Did I flip the tractor?

Should I call for help?

No.

No?

No. Don't call for help.

Why not call for help?

No. Feels risky somehow.

All right, no. Listen to your gut, my mom always says. And I do. It usually steers me right.

Okay, now what? How do I figure out where I am? Time for my left hand to do some exploring. Weird how I'm thinking about my left hand like it is a separate person from me, a friend I can rely on.

I reach out to touch the metal I felt before. It is a solid sheet, not far above my head. I trace a diamond-plate pattern with my fingertips. The farm has two tractors; both are smooth steel all over, except for the dirty roughness of the bucket. My tractor-accident theory is looking less likely.

A few inches later and the metal makes a right-angle turn away from me—and my hand hits the dirty shavings. Only my head is underneath this thing. Whatever it is, it protected me from being smothered to death.

Time to search my left side. Shavings. Manure. Hay. But then, close beside me, a pole of well-worn wood. I can feel the barely there ridges of grain in the oak. Pitchfork handle. This definitely feels like a pitchfork handle. I must be at the ranch. Where is there diamond-plate metal on the farm? I can't remember.

My left hand keeps going. The tips of my fingers touch more metal. This is something different, though. It's rough and flaky with rust. I slide my hand along the old steel. It has a soft curve. Like a bowl. But it's weird. Like the bowl is sort of shaking. It makes no sense.

I reach out as far as I can, but lose contact with the metal. Searching higher, my fingers touch metal again. A little hook. Odd. Then a straightaway of more metal. Then another metal hook. Another straightaway. Another hook.

I run out of arm. I am small and don't have much length of arm to work with. So I trace the hooks and the straightaways back to the thing that's like a bowl.

This all feels familiar. Those metal hooks remind me of my dad tying down a tarp in the bed of his truck.

A truck.

I am in the bed of a truck!

Why am I in the bed of a truck?

I reach out again for the metal hooks. Something tickles my hand.

Wind.

Stretching as far as I can go, I feel it in earnest now—the wind buffeting the skin of my hand. The wind, hard and fast.

This truck is moving.

How can that be? How can I be in a moving truck?

I reach out again, to check if I'm hallucinating. No. It's there; that biting, slapping wind is there. This truck is going fast. Then I feel the hum through my body. The hum in my ears isn't just concussion. It's a combination of engine and vibration. It's metal movement.

The diamond-plated thing above me must be a truck-bed toolbox. My head is in the empty space beneath it, protecting me from the shavings, keeping me alive.

I know where I am now.

I'm in the bed of a fast-moving truck, covered in blood, buried in filth. My right arm might be broken. I can't see.

Realization dawns, and I pull my hand in like I touched fire.

Fear slides into my belly as I wait.

Was I seen? Did someone see my hand?

The truck shift gears. It's slowing down. Quickly.

brazen (adj) 厚颜无耻的.
brazen out 厚着脸对待.
subtle (adj) 微妙的,敏感的.
trace (vt) 追踪,(n) 痕迹.

THE BOY SITS DOWN TO WAIT. OVER THE LAST HOUR HE'S put away his toys, tidied the house, put a Swanson TV dinner in the oven. Coffee is ready to brew. Ate his peanut butter sandwich and wiped away the crumbs. Everything is perfect.

After a few minutes of sitting on the couch he digs into his Snoopy book bag. Pulls out a math test with a B+ circled in red in the upper right hand corner. He's finally gotten the hang of carrying the one. He studies the paper. It might be worth the risk, putting it out where it could be seen. Maybe she'd be proud. But just as likely she'd say he was prideful. There was no right answer with her, as his uncle Lou liked to say. And Uncle Lou was her twin brother, so he'd know.

He tries it out on the kitchen table. Time ticks. No, it's too brazen out there, obviously wanting to be looked at like that. The boy moves it to the counter. That's definitely better. At least it's something close to subtle.

Returning to the couch to stare at the door, he drags his fingers through his thick, black hair. Sweat traces his hairline. She's late. Not necessarily a bad sign. Late, early, or on time makes no difference as to whether she comes home funny. But the later she is, the more waiting there is to be done. Only good thing is, the wait ends sharp as a snap. One look will tell him what he's in for.

Too much time has passed, and the boy loses his nerve. Leaving the test out is a bad idea; he knows that now. There can't be much time left, so it's a sprint to the counter. He grabs the sheet and hustles back to his book bag in the living room, but the front door is already opening. This isn't good. It's no good to be caught in quick motion.

He looks up and up and up to get to her face. His mama's a tall lady, and he's only seven. He's overwhelmed by red. Red heels, red nails, red lips, red hair, red eyes. So help him, the boy has always thought his mama's copper-colored eyes damn near shined red. He looks into those eyes and knows she's come home funny.

barn (n.) 谷仓

heave (n) 举起 (vt) 举起, 投掷.

Saddle (n) 马鞍. (vt) 承受.

Praise (n) 赞扬.

bungee (n) 蹦极, 橡皮筋.

Cord (n) 绳索, (vt) 用绳子捆绑.

Vomit (vt) 吐出 (n) 呕吐.

THE TRUCK SHIFTS UNDER ME. IT'S TURNING, TAKING a left. A moment of slow, smooth driving, and then the truck tips downward, lowering itself onto a gravel road. It must be nothing but potholes, because the truck tilts up and down and side to side like a theme-park ride. I fight hard against my stomach, against the vomit that wants to come up.

I wonder if I know this road, try to remember a road this rough, but come up empty. I try to think of who might be driving this truck. I try to remember how I got here.

All of my questions are answered by silence. Into the void comes a clear, single thought.

I've been abducted.

Once the thought comes, I have to look it in the face, and for the first time in my seventeen years I know what fear actually is.

It doesn't seem like this should be possible. My grandpapa has been telling me since I was a three-year-old to watch out for myself. Because he's not just my grandpapa, but also the sheriff, he didn't leave it at don't take candy from strangers. Ever the law-man, Grandpapa got specific. Usually at our after-church Sunday brunch, for some reason.

"Don't ever let them take you to a second location," he'd say in his low, slow, Johnny Cash intonation.

"You fight like hell!" Nana would pipe in. "You bite and you claw and you kick. You kick them where it hurts them the most! Go for the eyes, the crotch, the instep."

"Ruth, you promise me you'll fight and scream and you won't let them take you?" Grandpapa would ask.

I would nod my head. "I promise."

It's a conversation that's been had around the Carver kitchen table a dozen times, thanks to Grandpapa's paranoia.

My mom would insist, "Nothing like that is going to happen around here." Mom is a professional horse trainer and a devout optimist.

My dad, pragmatic, dryly funny, would end the conversation with "May God have mercy on the soul of the poor bastard who ever dared try it."

And then Nana and Grandpapa and even Mom would all smile.

"Our Ruth is a fighter," they always told me. They're not wrong, either. I am a fighter, born and raised. We Carvers aren't a family; we're a clan. We've lived on the same land, raising cattle and horses for three generations, and everybody in Mauldin knows you don't mess with the Carvers.

But here I am. In this truck. Did I fight? I don't know. My memory bank is empty. I can't even remember the last thing I can remember. What I know for certain is that I failed Grandpapa. I'd promised him I wouldn't let this happen to me, and I failed him. I'm not the fighter they thought I was.

A sob wants to come up my throat, but I won't let it. It's important to focus. Who would want to take me? My first thought is Creepy Kyle, my stalker since the eighth grade. My parents got involved; his parents got involved; the principal got involved. But I can't imagine Creepy Kyle getting the better of me, ever. I'm not scared of him and never have been.

A political opponent of Grandpapa's? Things get contentious in South Carolina politics, but that's hard to imagine.

Ransom? Mom and Dad have money. But not ransom-level money.

Creepy Kyle seems the most likely, yet not likely enough. I want to be able to see, to know where I am, to see who has me. My eyes don't seem painful. A hopeful sign. Slowly I reach for them again. My fingertips touch the bloody roughness.

The hard squeal of brakes, then a sudden stop. An avalanche of muck covers my face.

A door opens.

Slams shut.

Only one door. That's better than two.

Footsteps in the gravel. They sound heavy. Too heavy to be

Creepy Kyle. Not good. Creepy Kyle would want to keep me alive, I think, but I don't know this person. I don't know anything about what this person wants with me.

Is a bullet about to rip through me? Is a knife about to punch me in the throat? Far from fighting, I play dead. Not really with any thought, just instinct. It's not a very good ploy, considering I was moving my arm a second ago.

Footsteps stop.

For a brief moment I can hear birdsong. It is beautiful.

The tailgate slams open.

Is this it? Is this the end?

I'm not ready. I'm not ready for the end.

The man climbs up into the bed of the truck. It sinks under his weight. Definitely not Creepy Kyle.

I feel hands—giant hands—plunge into the dirt and pluck me out of it like a rag doll. My nose hits the toolbox on the way up. I manage to keep my mouth shut, but it's hard to play dead. My body won't go limp like I want it to. It's shaking, my nervous system giving me away. I give up the pretense.

"Who are you?" My voice sounds rusty, like I haven't spoken in years.

Nothing.

"Who are you?" I ask again.

The man throws me over his shoulder. Searing pain explodes out of my right arm. I scream.

"Shut up." His voice is unrecognizable to me.

I do. I shut up. I don't fight. I don't scream. Shame rides alongside my terror. But somewhere deep, deep inside, I hear Mom tell me to trust my gut. My gut tells me I am blind and I am lost, and if I fought for freedom now, it would end in my death. I listen to my gut. Because I want to live.

A truck door opens with a loud creak. He throws me inside. My hands fall against the bench seat. It is frayed and torn. Foam cushion blooms from the tears. The air isn't clean. It smells like mildew and rot. This is an old truck.

He grabs my wrists and doesn't let go. Neither does the agony of my shoulder; it digs in deep, teaching me what pain really is. He's tying my hands together, but it's not rope, it's a bungee cord. Only a bungee cord could be this tight.

"It's going to cut off my circulation. I'm going to lose my hands."

Nothing.

He binds my ankles. It's another bungee. I can feel the stretch, hear the slight click of the hooks coming together. The door slams shut. The tie around my legs is not nearly as bad as the one around my wrists. My cowboy boots help protect me. I am definitely wearing boots. So I was at the barn. What happened? Who is this? When is this?

There's somewhere else I'm supposed to be, but it's misty. A far-off location, and I'm supposed to be there, but I can't remember what it is. Fog. It's all a fog. I'm blind and confused and in trouble beyond what I thought possible.

I don't understand why this is happening to me. I'm a good person. A good daughter. A good friend. A decent student. And I work like hell. Nobody I know my age works as hard as I do. I'm at the ranch morning, afternoon, and night, working the farm, working Tucker, doing everything I possibly can to keep the farm on top, because winning isn't just winning. Not for me. For me, winning at the horse shows is required.

The cab of the truck leans toward the driver's side as the man gets in. He closes the door. I'm waiting for the sound of the gear shift, but the truck continues to idle. There, in that moment of stillness, something reaches me. A smell. It's familiar. A kind of cologne. I've smelled it before.

"Who are you?"

He answers with a blinding crack to my temple.

I'm dreaming, but at the same time I know I'm dreaming. But it's not really a dream. It's a memory. I'm at the barn. I'm uncomfortable. Someone is there I don't like.

Then I remember him. He is tall and big, with a large, black beard and bushy eyebrows. He has strange, hazel-orange eyes. He reminds me of a wolf.

He watches me while I tack up Tucker. I'm short and Tucker's tall. The man comes over and offers to help me heave the saddle onto Tucker's back. I don't say a word, but if looks could kill, he'd be dead. As offensive as the offer of help was, far worse is the watching.

A friend of Dad's from church recommended him, said he needed a second chance. He worked on the cattle side of the farm. Everybody sang his praises. He showed up on time, worked hard. But the guys who worked the cattle side of the operation had no business showing up at the horse barn. Most of them I never saw at all. But I kept seeing that wolf-looking guy, and that wolf-looking guy kept seeing me. I told Dad to fire him. He didn't want to, not at first, but then I explained how he watched me, and he was gone the next day.

That was all a long time ago. I can't recall his name, but I'll never forget that disgusting cologne.

With a jerk, I'm awake. I'm sitting on a wooden chair. My hands are bound behind my back, my feet to the chair legs. My fingers feel like swollen sausages that don't want to move. The bungee cord has done its work. I try to open my eyes, but it's no use. My eyelids are fastened shut. A stench, almost like the smell of a Dumpster, fills my nostrils. Under the stink there's mildew. Under the mildew there's dust. The kind of dust that comes from years and years of neglect. The dust and the mildew and the stink are so thick I can feel them on my skin.

I listen.

There's nothing to hear.

"Hello?"

Nothing.

Somehow silence is worse than sound. Is he right in front of me? Staring at me? The nausea comes again. This time I can't choke it back. I vomit down my shirt.

Concussion, I hate you.

"Hello?"

Nothing.

Panic wells up inside me, overriding reason. I have to get free.

I have to get free *now.* I wriggle and twist my numb hands. My right arm is screaming, but I don't care. It needs to suck it up. Like a miracle, one of the hook ends snaps off the bungee. In an instant my hands are free. Blood rushes into them. They move. They even work.

For a brief moment I listen. More silence. But this is good silence. If he were right there, staring at me, surely he would have done something by now.

Encouraged, I put my hands to my face and realize my arm isn't broken. Good news. It's not working well, but well enough that I can use it. With all ten fingers at my disposal, I examine my face and almost weep with relief. It's a vet-wrap blindfold. The clingy, neon pink bandage I've been using on Tucker's injured hoof. I'm not blind. I'm just bound.

It's never easy to find the end of vet wrap, and right now it's almost impossible. In the past I've had nothing but appreciation for how it molds onto the body like a second skin. I claw at it, desperate. Find the source of my concussion, a deep gash across the top of my scalp. A tear forms in the bandage, giving me leverage. Wolfman must have used an entire roll on my head.

There, it's off. I can open my eyes.

I'm in a small cabin.

Garbage covers everything. Moldering pizza boxes, cans of beer so old the sun has bleached the labels, rags soaked in gun oil.

I work on freeing my feet while glancing up every couple of seconds. I don't see him anywhere. Thick, ugly curtains obscure most of the view, but I can catch glimpses of a forest thick with pine and mountain laurel, rhododendron and muscadine vines. I'm in the Blue Ridge, maybe even the Great Smoky Mountains. I am far, far from home.

On my feet now, my body running on panic like it's rocket fuel, I check the front door. It's barred shut from the outside.

I check the back pocket of my jeans. My phone is gone. As I search for a side door, I remember where I'm supposed to be. It's fall break, and I should be at the beach with Courtney and Becca.

I find a side door. It's solid and barricaded, like the front.

We were going to meet up at Becca's house, then road-trip over to her dad's place on the coast. They have to have missed me by now, called my parents. Called Caleb. Oh, my redneck best friend Caleb, God bless you and your obscene collection of hunting rifles.

Yes, people will be out searching for me.

Not here, though. No one will think to look for me here.

It doesn't matter. I'll live in the woods if I have to. Find my way to a highway. Find my way to the people looking for me.

There are no other doors. Time to break something. I choose the back wall's lowest window, use my good arm to grab my wooden chair, and heave it through the glass. The amount of noise it makes shocks me. I kick out the remaining shards, then scramble through. It's a bigger drop than I anticipated, but I don't pause, launching myself out of the godforsaken cabin. After a bad stumble, I pop up to my feet and I'm ready to run.

The smoky smell hits me first.

A campfire.

I look up.

The Wolfman is right there, cooking meat over an open fire.

Five Years Ago

HER PARENTS ARE FIGHTING ABOUT MONEY AGAIN.

The girl is in a stall, standing ankle deep in clean shavings, pretending to brush her immaculate horse. She stands behind him, using him as a blind. She can't see her parents, and they can't see her. But she can't shut out sound.

The conflict is in perpetual motion, never ceasing. She's used to the fighting, desensitized, like a horse that's been made to walk over a tarp over and over again until it's no longer scared. But somehow, when she wasn't looking, hope for peace made its way through the cracks again, looking for the sun and a place to bloom. The hope came back because the girl had qualified for Worlds. All that money spent on horse shows had paid off, and they were here now, in Oklahoma City.

The fight began upon arrival. They learned they'd been assigned a stall in Barn 5A, far from everything. It didn't bother the girl. What did a few hundred feet matter when you were at Worlds? The best barns were dominated by the famous pro trainers with their curtains and potted plants and fountains and golf carts. The girl had one horse, one class to compete in, and her mother was her trainer. Of course they were stuck in no-man's-land.

But she knows their agitation over Barn 5A has nothing to do with her. It's a symbol of her mom's failure to make a lasting success of her early triumphs. She should be a big-deal trainer by now, with big-deal clients and big-deal horses. Instead, all her students are local kids taking riding lessons on the weekends. Every year the horse side of the ranch loses money. Lots and lots of money.

The girl understands all that.

But she can't help wishing that qualifying had been good enough. She'd allowed herself to hope that making it to Worlds as a twelve-year-old on a three-year-old horse would be enough to make them happy. It feels painfully naive in retrospect.

The horse turns to look at the girl. He is big and sweet and compliant, but she's been brushing the same spot on his shoulder for ten minutes, and his skin is irritated.

"I'm sorry, Tucker," the girl whispers. She shifts down a foot, turning her attention to his back, and he sighs, content once more.

Even quieter, she whispers to herself, "Just go away, go away, go away." She doesn't need to be that quiet. They can't hear her.

CHAPTER THREE

NOW IS NO TIME TO HESITATE AND I DON'T. I BOLT AWAY from the cabin, ignoring the pain in my pumping right arm, ignoring my churning stomach. Racing past the Wolfman, I risk a glance in his eyes and see nothing. Not surprise, not worry, not urgency, not even anger. They're empty. Far emptier than any animal's eyes. Those empty eyes, more than anything, frighten me into running faster. Faster than I ever thought I could run.

And I'm fast.

But something catches my foot.

A root? Dear God, no, not a root. Did I trip on a root?

I look back.

No, my foot is in his hand. He's flat out on his stomach; he worked for it, but still—how did he do that? How could such a big man move so fast? Bafflement gives way to raw terror as he pulls me to him.

I start screaming no. I hear myself scream. Over and over again I scream no, but it's like someone else is moving my mouth, making my voice box work. He tells me to shut up, but the words are from another world. He puts his hand over my mouth.

The feel of his hand touching my face brings my mind and my brain back together, and I bite him. Hard.

He grabs my throat with his other hand.

With one finger pointing in my face, he says, "Stop."

I bite him again.

"If you don't stop, I squeeze until you die."

He gives me a sample. He's not wrong. He will squeeze until I die. I don't even think it would be hard for him. Not on any level.

"Will you stop?"

I nod yes.

He takes me by the nape of my neck and drags me toward his campfire. My face is shoved into leaf litter and black mountain soil as he fetches his steak, one-handed. The sounds of sizzling meat, clinking utensils, and tinfoil are strangely homey. He heaves me to my feet, and his strength overwhelms me yet again. I watch, feeling helpless, as he casually kicks dirt into the fire to snuff it out. How responsible of him.

Once done, he pulls me back toward the cabin's front door. I glance around as we walk. I see no signs of a real road anywhere nearby. No other houses. No sounds. There's nothing here but forest, the moss-eaten cabin, and the old truck out front. Now that I can see it, I remember that truck. Peeling red paint, rust. Late-seventies Chevy.

Wolfman undoes the barricade on the front door and shoves

me into the cabin. Just as quick, he whirls me around to face the rudimentary kitchen. As I spin, I catch sight of something important. Keys hanging on a small nail next to the front window.

In one smooth motion, he pushes me into a chair at the little kitchen table, sets down his steak, and picks up a gun. I wish with all my might I'd seen the gun before he picked it up. But I didn't know it was there, hidden in the mountains of trash, and he moved so quickly. I lost my chance, and now I'm staring down the barrel of a stout-looking .45. He sits down opposite me.

I still can't remember his name.

Silence. He watches me. I want to look down, block my eyes from his, but it's too important that I learn all I can. His face is impassive, his body a hulking granite boulder, but his hands are trembling. That more than anything scares me. A part of me wants him to speak, break the tension of the quiet. The other part of me wants him to never say anything.

"I want you to know something," he says. His eyes may be empty, but his voice is full. He's saying something he thinks is important. "I did not want to come back here. Do you understand me?"

I have no idea what I should say. "I don't think I do."

"I didn't want to come back here. I'd stopped coming. Do you understand me?"

There's impatience behind his words, but I think pretending to understand will only make things worse. "I don't."

"I've been clean for a long time. Made a promise to myself, more importantly, made a promise to somebody else. I hate to tell you this, because you're already so high on yourself." He pauses for emphasis, and then I hear the rage. "So damn high on yourself."

This man hates me in a way I didn't know was possible. Another wave of adrenaline floods my system, and it's like my body is overwhelmed, put into slow motion. Every second is longer, more frozen.

"But sometimes things need to be done and promises need to be broken. And so here we are."

"We don't have to be here," I offer.

He points at me, like an angry principal. "You have to learn that you're not special."

"I don't think I'm special."

He smacks me hard across the face. I had no idea his arm was long enough to reach across the table.

"No lying."

A weird whining fills my ears, and my body goes from slow motion to hyperkinetic freak-out. My heart, my sweat, my nerves, my muscles all burst to life and frantically move in place. There's nowhere to go, but everything squirms and writhes inside me, as though individual bits of me are trying to escape.

"What I'd like to know is, how come a little girl like yourself is in charge of business decisions at a multimillion-dollar facility?"

I almost protest, but Wolfman said no lying. "I'm not in charge, but I have input because I bring a lot of money into the farm. I'm our best advertisement."

"Some things you're in charge of. You're the sole voice of authority."

There's a vague feeling I'm missing something important, that

I'm not thinking clearly through all the stress. "I manage the girls who feed at the barn, teach them how and make sure they do it right. I guess I'm in charge of that."

"You're also in charge of who gets fired at a moment's notice. Or did your daddy lie when he said you made the call to fire me?"

A strange melting sensation happens inside me. How could my father be so stupid?

"He said you thought I wasn't right, that I scared you. Was he lying?" Wolfman raises his right hand, ready to strike. "Was he lying?"

"No."

"So you agree you are in charge. Do you think it's right, for a little girl to be in charge like that?"

It's a strange question for me to hear and harder for me to process.

"Answer. Do you think you should be in charge?"

"I'm trying."

Another crack across the head. This one is worse. "You're not trying! You're not saying anything. Do you think you should be in charge?"

"Yes!" He's reopened the wound on my scalp. Blood trickles into my eyes, so I squeeze the lids shut tight. "Because there's nobody else."

There's a long pause. That second hit has me spinning around even as I sit still. My closed eyes are only making it worse, but there's a steady drip of blood. I open them, not wanting to vomit.

Through the red haze of my blood I see a strange expression on his face. His eyes have come alive, and I don't like it at all. He's getting off on this now in a way he wasn't before. My first thought is that my honesty is feeding him in a bad, bad way, and my second thought is not to question my gut.

"These are going to be very good days," he says to me.

An hour has passed without conversation. I watched Wolfman eat his steak and drink can after can of cheap beer. He doesn't seem drunk, but there's a blurriness about his eyes that disturbs me. It feels like he's getting ready to enjoy something.

Anxiety wants to take me over, but I fight it back. I think I learned something in our first conversation. He wants to break me down, get to the core of me. My truth is his crack. No more of that. No more playing this game by his rules. From now on he'll know only what I want him to know. From now on I stay in control. That's what's going to get me out of here.

Wolfman clears everything off the table except his gun. That he keeps close at hand. There is a sense of ceremony about his actions. My stomach tightens up. We are about to begin.

From the back of his jeans he retrieves two objects. One is a mini spiral-bound notebook. The other is my cell phone. He then pulls a pair of foldable reading glasses from his shirt pocket. He puts them on, letting them rest low on his nose, and uses both hands to flip through the notebook. The notebook is nearly filled with neat, tiny print, and it takes some time for him to find what he's looking for.

Once he's found his spot, he pauses to look at me over his glasses. This is clearly a planned performance, but he's trying to pull off an air of spontaneity. "I think you're going to be my hardest case yet. But you will learn in the end. They all do."

Hardest case yet. I'm not the first. I already knew this, and yet hearing it said so starkly sends a surge of bile up my throat. I swallow hard to keep from gagging.

"I know you, Ruth Ann Carver. I know you better than you know yourself. You think you do things right. You think you're a paragon of right living. This is a self-told lie, one bolstered by your coddling parents and grandparents."

A spike of rage joins my fear. Say what you want about me, but nobody speaks ill of my family.

"Your *coddling* parents and grandparents," he says again, "who shelter you from the truth. Now, I'm a reasonable man, and do not expect you to simply take my word for it."

His gaze returns to the little notebook. He clears his throat and begins reading. "'Nine a.m. on October seventh. Young blond girl asks for help with horse. Target replies, "I don't have time for you. In this barn, you either sink or swim."'"

His strange wolf eyes bear into mine, searching for my reaction. I don't want to feel ashamed; I don't want to feel anything. I want to stay in strict control. But I do remember saying that. The girl, Natalie, wouldn't stop pestering me. If I stopped to help her every time she asked for help, I wouldn't get my own work done.

"'Nine thirty a.m. on October seventh. Young blond girl goes to the other teens to complain about Target. Other teens say, "Don't worry about Ruthless."'"

I had no idea they called me that. It doesn't entirely surprise me. What's hitting me harder is the label he's given me: Target.

"They went on to say that you weren't nice to anyone, cared only about winning, and had no friends."

But I *do* have friends. Not many. Mostly just Becca and Courtney, because Becca swims and Courtney plays soccer, and they know what it is to give your life to your sport. But it's not like we never have fun. We do. We just put our sports first. And there's Caleb. I'll always have my Caleb.

"They went on to tell the young blond girl to stick with them, as they all have fun together at the horse shows, root each other on, and ignore you."

Which is fine by me. I don't go to competitions to play around. I go to win.

"'Nine forty-five a.m. on October seventh. Target's mother walks in on conversation. Young blond girl relays Target's words. Target's mother says, "It's my fault she's nasty. Blame me."'"

Again he looks to me, waiting to see my expression. I do everything I can to keep my face set, but my cheeks grow warm, something he can probably see. My pale, freckly skin glows like a neon light when I blush. Would Mom really say that? It can't be the truth. She wouldn't sell me out like that.

"'Eight a.m. on October eighth. Target's mother asks Target's father to talk to Target about the way she treats riding students at the barn. Target's father says, "It's not worth getting into World War Three over. You know how she is; if she thinks she's right, she'll fight to the death, and she always thinks she's right. You try dealing with her this time. See how you like it.'"'

Do my parents really talk like this behind my back? I don't want to believe Dad would say those things. It especially hurts that he said it where this man could hear him. He let this hired hand, this monster, know exactly what he thought of me. But I do believe it, because it makes sense. He's always the one who talks to me, and I always defend myself. I just didn't know he considered me such a burden.

"'Four p.m. on October tenth. Caleb helped Target (at her request) with chores for several hours. Then he wanted her company. Target asked him to leave and then complained to the mother that he had overstayed his welcome. Target is a user.'"

But Caleb will stay forever if I don't ask him to leave! We're best friends; I help him out too. Sometimes. I'll help if he asks for it, anyway. It's always been like this. This is how we are.

The Wolfman picks up my cell phone. "I found this to be of interest." He holds up the phone and shows a picture of me and Becca at her mom's pool. We're in bikinis. "You sent this photo to Caleb. And also this one, and this, and this," he says, scrolling down. "You use him whenever you're feeling insecure. You know he is going to tell you you're beautiful. You know Caleb's feelings go beyond friendship and use this knowledge to your advantage. I suspect you have feelings for him, but you'd never date him. You're ashamed of him because he's a redneck and lives in a trailer."

I don't know how the Wolfman knows all this, but he's not wrong. My warm cheeks turn scalding hot.

"Your shame is a good sign. You may break sooner than I thought. The breaking is good. It purifies."

He's getting inside my head. I can't let him get inside my head.

"Look down," Wolfman says.

I look at the floor.

"Not that low. Look at the table. There's a drawer in it. Right in front of you. Open it."

The last thing on earth I want to do is open it. I don't want to know what's in there.

"Open it."

I'm so frightened of what's in that drawer I think I'm going to throw up again. Using my left hand, I open the drawer.

Cards. Playing cards.

"Count them. See if there are fifty-two."

Somehow this surreal twist makes it all worse. I don't want to be played with. He's the cat and I'm the mouse.

"Count them and see if there are fifty-two."

He picks the gun up and cocks it.

As I count the cards, a question beats against the inside of my head, until I can't stop the words from spilling out of me.

"Why me?" I ask. "Why'd you start following me?"

"Whenever I spot a redhead, I take a good, long look."

It's so ridiculous, I find myself saying, "Are you kidding me?"

For several seconds I do nothing but blink. That I have red

hair, of all things, would be what led me to this place feels so outrageously unfair, my sense of injustice momentarily outweighs the shock and horror of my situation.

"You were on thirty-two."

I return to counting cards. When I finish, there are fifty-two cards stacked in front of me. "Fifty-two," I say.

"I knew there were fifty-two. This was an exercise in obedience. I'm glad to see you're learning to comply."

I can't stop myself from pointing out the obvious. "You're pointing a gun at me."

He smiles again. "This is the sort of redheaded feistiness I expected."

"Maybe I'm feisty, but not all redheads are feisty."

"So far, all of you have been feisty."

How many have there been?

My breathing quickens. I fight to control it. No good showing weakness. Have to be strong, but these references to other victims are unnerving. I look around the cabin, searching for evidence of the other girls brought here before me.

"Keep your eyes on the cards."

I do as I'm told.

"Now deal 'em out."

"How many?"

"Seven for each of us."

As I deal out cards, he picks up my phone.

"Let's see if you have any new text messages," Wolfman says. "Here's one from Mom: 'Glad to hear you got to Becca's okay.

Drive carefully, and tell her dad we said hello.'" He navigates to the next text. "This one is from Becca: 'So sorry you're sick. It'll be hard to have fun without you, but we'll try!'"

I sit at the table, frozen. No one knows I'm gone. No one is searching for me. No one has any idea I'm missing. I'm alone. I'm all alone in this.

Forty-Three Years Ago

IT'S MAY IN THE DEEP SOUTH, AND THE AIR INSIDE THE sixth-grade classroom is stifling. The girls wear thin cotton dresses; the boys are in short sleeves. In the very back a tall, husky, black-haired boy wears an old green jacket that doesn't fit right. The jacket looks a bit like Little Joe Cartwright's, but nobody watches Bonanza anymore. Except the boy. He watches Bonanza.

The jacket is zipped up tight, compressing his belly into a too-small space. Heat radiates from his cheeks; he can feel them throb in time with his pulse. Dark green mushroom clouds of sweat have formed under his armpits and on his back. The stains are worrisome. They might call attention to him, and the boy's singular goal is to get through this day unnoticed.

With every sense on high alert for predators, he has nothing to spare for such trivialities as the math lesson going on at the front of the classroom.

"Jerry?"

A handful of students pivot to hear his response, but to him it feels like the entire world has turned.

"Ma'am, I didn't have my hand up."

"I realize that. Please order these fractions from least to greatest."

"Ma'am, I really didn't have my hand up."

The teacher walks toward him. More heads turn. Perversely, she wears a long tweed skirt, but not a bead of sweat. Her pale hair, the same color as her face, is perfectly teased into a hair-sprayed helmet. Now five feet from the boy, she scrunches her drawn-on eyebrows in concern.

"Jerry, what on earth is going on? You look sick."

"Yes, ma'am, I think I am. Can I go to the restroom?"

"You may."

Jerry jumps up. Growth spurts have hit him hard, and he stumbles over the legs of his desk. Some of the jackals titter. It's a headlong tumble for the door, but he's forced to stop before he can make his escape.

"Jerry, when you come back, I want you in short sleeves! Don't know what you're thinking, wearing that jacket."

He pauses. How can he agree to this?

"You hear me? Short sleeves. It's ridiculous, you wearing that on a day like this."

"Yes, ma'am."

In the empty hallway the boy opens his locker, his movements frantic. He takes off his jacket; he is shirtless underneath. From the locker he pulls out a plain white T-shirt. Plain except for a handwritten message, scrawled in ballpoint pen.

I WET THE BED.

He turns the shirt inside out, which obscures the print somewhat, then puts the shirt on back to front. The tag is now beneath his neck. Grabbing it with his teeth, he tries to rip it off. The tag is stitched in tight. He puts his head into his locker, digging around for a compass, a pair of scissors, anything sharp.

He doesn't hear the footsteps behind him until it's too late.

"I wet the bed?"

And then giggles.

He flings his back to the wall of lockers with a mighty clang. Three girls have semicircled him. They're seventh-grade girls. Popular girls. They giggle like seagulls ripping apart a crab.

"Is that what your shirt says?" asks the redhead. She speaks with a cold authority.

"No," he lies.

"Let me see!" squeals the prettiest brunette. She grabs his shoulder and tries to pull him forward. He's a head taller than her and a lot stronger. His back stays pressed against the metal lockers.

The less pretty brunette is rough, aggressive. "C'mon! Show her!"

"Is it true?" asks the redhead. "Do you wet the bed? Do you?"

The less pretty brunette pulls on his other shoulder. She's an athlete and makes some headway. The boy's planted feet squeak on the linoleum.

The redhead keeps up her simple interrogation. "Do you wet the bed? Do you?"

"No!" He's panicked now. The brunettes are too close to success. The redhead doesn't move a muscle. She's in charge of giggling and asking questions.

The less pretty brunette grabs the front of the boy's shirt and pulls with everything she has, forcing him off balance. He takes a stagger-step forward, and the pretty brunette seizes the moment, pushing her foot against the back of his knee. The boy's leg buckles. One more shirt tug sends him to the floor.

"See! It does *say he wets the bed! You wet the bed! You wet the bed!"*

He looks up, and something crystallizes within his brain. He is bigger than them. He is stronger than them. He should be the boss of them.

The boy bursts from the floor with his right fist raised, catching the redhead under her chin with such force she's knocked out cold. His next motion is to grab the pretty brunette. She tries to run away, but her long hair is easily caught. She's ripped off her feet, and a second later she rolls on the floor, grabbing her head and crying. A small fist cracks the boy across the cheek. It's the less pretty brunette, scrappier than her fellows by half. Her punch only serves to further enrage him.

When he unleashes on her, everything falls together. Like a crick in the neck snapped into place, the boy's brain pops and is put right. It is a beautiful undoing, a beautiful becoming. He doesn't stop to think about it when the punches follow her down to the ground. He doesn't stop to notice when she goes still or when the pool of blood under her head pillows out into a great, liquid heart. He doesn't stop until he's pulled off her, and he doesn't start to think again until that night, when he's back at home. For hours and hours his brain stays beautifully popped into place.

CHAPTER FOUR

I'M FROZEN, THINKING OF MY PARENTS, WHO BELIEVE I'm with my friends, and my friends, who believe I'm with my parents. My shock pleases the Wolfman. I can see it in his face.

He says, "Why'd you stop dealing? Seven to both of us."

As I deal the cards, I pray. *Dear God. Help me. Please help me. Please, God, help me.*

"Caleb's texts made for interesting reading. Not too bright, is he?"

"He's smart; he's just dyslexic. That's why he can't spell. But he's smart."

"Not smart enough to get away from you."

His mockery of Caleb makes me angry. "And neither are you, apparently," I say.

He likes my threat, thinks it's cute. "You really are the toughest case yet. You haven't even cried." With relish he adds, "This is going to take some work."

There's a disturbing undercurrent of perversion beneath those words. So far he's been oddly rational, under control. But I know I'm not here to play cards and be lectured to. I'm here to be purified, and it doesn't take a rocket scientist to realize that the purification he has planned will defile and destroy me, and eventually leave me dead.

I want to get back to cards and lectures. "And now there's seven cards dealt. What are we playing?"

"It's a game I invented. If you win, we keep playing. If you lose, we play a new kind of game. The record holder is seven games won. But she lost in the end, of course. They all do."

It is evident that I don't want to move on to whatever the "new kind of game" might be. "What are the rules?"

"The goal is to get the queen of hearts." He pauses. "I call it the Virgin Queen."

There it is. His rational veneer has slipped, exposing his slimy underbelly, and now the cards really are out on the table. I bark out a laugh and pray it sounds authentic. "If that's what you thought you're getting, I hate to break it to you, but I'm no virgin."

I'm lying. But I figure, if it's virgins he wants, it'll be sluts he hates. I have nothing against sluts, personally. I try to channel Rachel, a girl from school who likes to brag about her conquests. She even once bragged about acquiring a disease. I call up our conversation. Not too hard, as it was a memorable one.

"Truth is, two weeks ago I had to go to Planned Parenthood.

Turns out it was trich. You ever heard of trich? It's not even a bacteria or a virus; it's a protozoa. A little animal." I try to nod knowingly, but it probably looks more like I'm having a seizure.

"You're lying."

"You wish I was lying." I ransack my fuzzy brain for a key detail from Rachel's story. Her antibiotic was the same thing we used when our dog had giardia. I visualize the label on Hooligan's pill bottle. There. I see it. "I'm taking metronidazole to clear it up, but I'm still contagious."

"You're lying. You've never even had a boyfriend."

How did he know that? My cheeks flush again. Few things embarrass me more than my lifelong lack of a boyfriend. With all the bravado I can muster I say, "Sluts don't have boyfriends."

Please, dear God, make me appear believable as a slut. Please, please let him think I'm a slut.

I peer into those strange eyes and I see doubt.

The cards sit before us. Unplayed.

A shrill ring blares out of nowhere, making us both jump. He stands, grabbing the gun with his left hand, and pulls a phone out of his front pocket with his right. I can't believe there's cell reception up here. Maybe we're not as far out into the middle of nowhere as I thought.

He answers his phone. After saying hello, he says "Yes, sir," several times, his tone polite and professional. He hangs up, returns the phone to his pocket. The Wolfman leans in to the kitchen counter, his back to me. His shoulders go up and down, up and down, and I realize it's his breathing, and that he's furious. Rage radiates out of him in waves. Fear overtakes me, makes me very still, makes me want to become invisible.

Wolfman explodes.

He attacks furniture, not me, but it takes everything I have to keep from crying at the sheer magnitude of his violence. I'm certain the gun will go off in the chaos, but somehow it doesn't. When he's done, a coffee table—which wasn't much to begin with—lies in pieces on the floor.

Drained, he turns to me. "I have to go to the plant." He pauses, shaking his head, and when he speaks, he's not really talking to me. "I'm supposed to have this week off. I did all the proper paperwork as soon as I knew. I should have this week. It can take a week to do it right." After a moment, he adds, "It's because I'm new." He sounds like a pouty child, but his ham-size fists clench and unclench, making me worry another attack is coming.

Summoning courage from somewhere, I say, "Well, just think. Perfect alibi." I'm hoping he'll think it's a feisty sort of thing to say. I'm hoping he'll be entertained into leaving this dangerous anger behind.

Instead, he roars. "Shut up, slut!"

I brace, waiting for a bullet, waiting to be assaulted.

"When I get back, we'll find out if you're a lying redhead or a befouled slut with no chance at redemption."

To me this sounds like a choice between being raped and murdered or just murdered.

"Get on the couch," he says, gesturing with the gun. "I have to tie you up before I go."

◆ ◆ ◆

When I wake up, I don't know where I am. All I know is that my head hurts with an intensity I've never felt before. My throat is like sandpaper. I'm dying of thirst. Maybe my headache is caused by dehydration. I open my eyes. It is dark.

Things come into focus. The moon must be full. Slats of pale light stream into the room.

I'm laid out on the couch, wrapped up in rope like a mummy. I'm on my stomach, my head twisted uncomfortably to the side. There is no sign of the Wolfman. Somewhere along the way I've soiled myself. It is disgusting. Exhaustion overwhelms me. Groping through memory, I recall the Wolfman coming at me with a white cloth. It smelled sickly sweet. Chloroform. Holding my breath, I did my best to take in as little of it as possible. Maybe I had some success. Maybe that's why I'm awake now.

Not that I'd call this situation a success.

My tongue is glued to the roof of my mouth. Working it free, I realize it's been a very long time since I ate, since I drank. Vaguely I wonder if the Wolfman's steak is on the counter. Then it comes back. He ate it already, in front of me.

The darkness tries to take over. It's seductive that way, luring me into itself. The excruciating pain in my head can't follow me down into the darkness. Neither can the stink of this place, the stink of me. The roughness of my tongue, the power of my thirst, none of it exists down there in the dark.

It'd be so easy, so pleasant, just to let go and fall into that darkness. To let it have me. It feels right there, so close, so delicious. All

I need to do is let go, give up, and there'd be peace. Peace and no more pain.

But what about Grandpapa? I promised him I'd fight. What about Nana and my parents? They'd want me to fight. But they don't know how tired I am. They don't know what this feels like. They don't know how impossible this is.

And I didn't do anything to deserve this.

I am a good person. I am a good person and I don't deserve this.

Then the Wolfman's notebook, his list of my sins, comes back to me. As much as I want to think those quotes were lies, I believe they're true. He got what I said right, and the comments from the other girls at the barn don't totally surprise me. I don't want it to, but it stings. I thought they respected me. Really, I thought they feared and respected me, and I liked it that way.

But my parents' words flat-out hurt. Maybe I'm not easy to be around, but I've never talked shit about them behind their backs. My loved ones have my loyalty, and my loyalty is something that doesn't break. Doesn't even bend. The family ranch gets all of me, every last bit of me. I've given it everything I have. Everything I have should be worth something. It should be worth their loyalty.

Of course, all these poisonous thoughts, they're based on the words of an evil man who tortures people for fun. Would he be smart enough to mix falsehoods in with the truth? Or twist my parents' words? Take them out of context? Maybe. It's hard to tell how smart he is. His weirdness makes him hard to read.

Except Caleb. Wolfman is right about that. I need to be better to Caleb. He deserves better than me. He deserves so much better than me. He never fails me; he's always there, no matter what. Year after year.

I open my eyes, mostly to blink away the tears. My gaze falls upon a pile of fabric on an end table. Under a thick layer of dust there are multiple patterns and colors. They come in and out of focus as I think about my past, the things I've done, who I am. If I'm honest with myself, I can see why the Wolfman says I'm arrogant and selfish and proud. I can see why people say I am cold, I am hard, and I am only interested in winning.

Maybe I deserve this. Maybe I should take it as my due. Maybe I should just give up and die. It would be easy, so beautifully easy. Muscles I didn't even know were tensed let go and relax, ready to let me slip away.

Before I give in to the darkness, a feeble voice fights back. It says: *No, I don't deserve this. Maybe I am a bad, horrible person, but this isn't right. No one deserves this. No one.*

I wake up to the bright light of day. Nothing has changed except now the sun shines. I still stare at the strange pile of fabrics on the small end table; I'm still tied up; I'm still on the couch. There's no sign of the Wolfman.

My thoughts from the night prior return to me. Am I perfect? No. Are there things I'd change about myself if I got the chance? Yes. But there's nothing wrong with being tough, with being a fighter, with being a winner. And my last thought before passing out was the right one: *No one deserves this.*

I breathe in deeply. The intensity of my headache has lessened a bit. The concussion is healing.

Time to start thinking again.

I blink to clear my eyes and my thoughts. The pile of fabrics on the end table comes into new focus, and I realize what I'm looking at. Panties. It's a pile of panties.

Signs of the girls who were here before me.

The shock of it sends me upright, and a second realization hits. I am tied head to toe like a mummy, but I am not tied down to anything else. In my fog I'd assumed I was stuck in place, unable to move. It takes energy and balance and strength, but I manage to get to my feet and shuffle over to the end table.

My left hand is hopelessly tied down, but my right fingers can wiggle free. Electric bolts of pain shoot up from my right hand to my shoulder. I ignore them. As I look down at the old, faded panties, a new horror fills me. I see a pair with rainbows on it. Another with pink cartoon flowers. These other girls, they were even younger than me. They were children.

Children.

A sense of purpose blooms. The Wolfman is right about me. He's right that I'm hard and driven and more than a little mean. He's right that I'm the hardest case he'll ever know. Because unlike these poor little girls who came before me, I'm old enough and strong enough to beat him. And God knows, if there's anybody on earth who knows how to win, it's me.

This is why I was abducted by this *thing*. I'm here to stop him. I'm here to make sure this never happens again.

I think back to the millions of lessons from my mom, back to our planning sessions before horse shows. Victory, as she has told me a thousand times, is found in the details and in setting goals.

"Here's how this is going to go down," I say to no one but myself and God. "Number one, I am not going to be raped. Number two, I am going to escape. Number three, I will see him brought to justice. That is how this is going to go down."

I touch the edge of the end table in homage to the victims who came before me, the victims who are in heaven. Bowing my head in prayer, I say, "Help me. Be my guardian angels. Let me do this. Let me do this for you. For us."

Breathing deep, I feel the presence of the others around me. I stay just as I am, head bowed, hand on the end table. Holding on to the feeling, I do nothing but take in the sensation that I am not alone, that they are going to help me, that they are going to be with me. The feeling passes, and my eyes focus on the rough wood floor of the cabin.

There's a line cut through the boards.

It isn't easy, tied up as I am, but I follow the line, scraping away the trash with my foot. The line meets up with another, then another, then another. There is a four-by-four square cut into this floor, cut to provide access to the ground below.

I tap the table. "You're down there, aren't you?"

It feels as though someone says yes.

I tap the table one more time.

Now.

Time to act.

I pivot toward the kitchen. I need a knife to cut these ropes. As I waddle forward, it occurs to me Wolfman might think I'm younger than seventeen, because I'm so small. He is used to dealing with terrified children who can't defend themselves. Why else would he not tie me to the couch? Unless it's a trap. He could be on the other side of a window watching me. Ready to punish me.

It's a risk I have to take. My hope is that he's become overconfident preying on children. He's about to find out I'm no child. Even so, the fear that he might come upon me, the fear that this is a trap, makes my hand tremble as I open kitchen drawers, searching for a knife.

I look out a window and listen. No sign of Wolfman or his truck. More drawers reveal nothing useful. Then, somewhere far, far away, a sound. My imagination? Maybe. Or maybe a chain saw miles away. But all the same the sound sends a shot of adrenaline into me.

More drawers, more nothing. Cabinets, now, but there's nothing I can use to free myself of this mummy rope.

The sound of the old truck's engine reaches my ears. *It's him.* Driving slowly on these mountain paths, but maybe not slowly enough.

Time to get back on the couch, act like I never moved. I quickstep as fast as I can, knowing that a fall would leave me exposed, vulnerable to punishment.

The truck door slams shut.

He's almost here.

I lie down on the couch, find the position he left me in, just as he unlocks the door. Turning my face toward the floor, I pretend to be asleep.

I pray he doesn't notice anything out of place.

Wolfman shuffles around the cabin. It's hard to tell what he's doing, but if he finds something infuriating—a drawer or a cabinet door left open—I'll hear about it pretty quick. As I cringe and wait like a beaten dog, my promise to the previous victims returns to me.

I will not be a victim. I will not think like a victim. I am going to avenge all those little girls. I am going to win.

More shuffling from Wolfman. I open one eye, the one closer to the couch. On the floor are several hunting magazines. And there, in the corner of each of them, a label with his name and address. I set about memorizing the information and hope to God I get a chance to use it.

Five Years Ago

ALL THE GIRL WANTS IS FOR HER PARENTS TO STOP FIGHTING and leave. Once they leave, she can call the boy who is like the other half of herself. It's been that way ever since he moved into the trailer on the Carver property. At first it was a whole family. A mom, a dad, two daughters, and a son. Then the dad left and the boy changed. He grew up in a hurry, becoming more of a man than his daddy ever was. The girl misses the free spirit the boy used to be, but at moments like this, she's grateful for his seriousness.

The girl is still in her horse's stall, still hiding from her parents. The fight stops. The clicking of cowboy boots on concrete announces the departure of her father.

"Ruth, I'm going to the show office." Her mom sounds tired, angry. "God knows it's five miles from here, so it'll be a while."

"Okay," the girl says, trying to sound normal.

She pulls her phone out of her back pocket. Her hand is shaking, and she feels betrayed by her own body. She never shakes like this. It takes two tries before she successfully calls the boy. The phone rings, and her throat closes up on her. What if she cries? The thought is horrifying. No one hears Ruth Carver cry. Not ever. Not even him.

"Hello?" He sounds concerned, as though he already knows something is wrong.

She can't say anything.

"Ruthie?"

Forcing a deep breath, she says, "Yes." Except she doesn't. It comes out as a gasp for air, a metallic hiss.

The boy's voice lowers. "Are they fighting?"

"Yes."

"Well, I guess it's the same old, same old."

All she can do is nod.

"Ruthie, what's the matter?"

"I can't speak," she whispers.

The boy is quiet, trying to figure out what has her this upset. "Is it worse than usual?"

"No, it's the same. It's exactly the same." The words come out with vehemence, frustration.

Something clicks for the boy. "And you thought going to Worlds was going to change things."

"Yes." Her "yes" is nothing but a humiliated husk of a word.

"Don't be embarrassed. There's nothing worse than getting your hopes up for nothing, especially when you have a whole heap of pressure on you."

"Thank you." His understanding is an exquisite relief.

"Look. Me and Ma will be there Saturday. We'll be there to watch you. Okay?"

"Okay." The girl feels a little better, knowing her best friend will soon be there.

"I'll say prayers for you. I'll tell Ma to say some prayers for you, too. She'll tell her small group and then you'll have a whole heap of people praying for you and rooting you on, okay?"

"Thanks, Caleb." A warm wash of love for the boy comes over her. His lack of judgment, his unwavering support, it all means so much.

"And, Ruthie, it ain't fittin' for them to fight in front of you like that; it ain't fittin' at all."

And just as quickly, that love disappears. Why does he have to talk like a redneck? He's smarter than that, should be better than that. It just shows why Caleb could never be a part of the Carver clan. The Carvers are about being the best. Caleb is so close to that, so close to great. But he's not. He's on the other side of the line.

"Thanks, Caleb," she says again, her voice cold. "I gotta go."

His redneck ways have always been an irritant, but now, in the moment when she most needs him to be perfect, it brings home everything that's wrong.

CHAPTER FIVE

THE WOLFMAN CONTINUES TO ROOT AROUND IN THE kitchen as I lie facedown on the couch. Address memorized, I stare at the hunting magazines. *Never in a million years would I have guessed his name was Jerry T. Balls.* What kind of a name is Jerry Balls? In a different world from this one it would be funny. Thing is, he doesn't look like a Jerry, and that name doesn't ring a bell. I can't remember what they called him when he worked for us, but it wasn't that. To me, he looks like a Wolfman. He will always be Wolfman to me.

His home address is two towns over from mine. If his plant job is around there, he's making one hell of a commute. No wonder I was alone for so long.

During our next card game it will be my goal to find out where this cabin is. Maybe even how far away from civilization. But first and foremost—food and water. I need to get some fuel into my body. Once I make my escape, I'll need all the energy I can get.

The heavy steps of Wolfman are coming closer. I tense, waiting; the nerves on the back of my neck prickle as he looms over me. So close his breathing ruffles my hair. His breath is sour.

He says, "You stink."

Out behind the cabin there is a garden hose, and I am being sprayed down with it. I'm naked. I'm freezing. My body convulses with cold. My underwear now sits on the end table with the rest. Everything in me wants to curl up, hide, cover my face. But it's not going to happen. Standing straight and tall, my eyes open and on the Wolfman's, I try to think about nothing but the water dripping down my face and pulling every little droplet into my mouth.

I'd hoped to get food before I left. I'd hoped to get more information and a kitchen knife. I'd hoped to maybe steal his truck. Those things didn't happen. This is what did, and this is what is important:

I am outside.

He didn't bring his gun.

But he did bring a whole new expression to his wolf eyes. He's done thinking, done planning, done preparing. Things are about to get real. I can feel it. I recite my goals. *Number one, I will not be raped. Number two, I will escape. Number three, I will bring him to justice.*

"Turn around and bend over."

My pulse quickens.

I turn very slowly, catch some of my red hair in my mouth

and suck the water from it. Bending over, I drink as quickly and as much as I can, even using my hands to cup the water. He says nothing. All the while I'm listening for even one footstep forward. These moments are precious. This water is precious.

Then the water becomes uneven. Instead of a steady spray against the back of my neck, it travels down my body, off it altogether, and then back to my neck.

Curious, I hang my head down and glance through the space between my ribs and my arm. He's masturbating. He had to juggle the hose and his zipper. That's why the spray of water didn't stay steady.

But it's not revulsion that strikes me. It's something else. I think:

This is good.

This is excellent.

Taking the tiniest steps, I inch away from him.

When I go, I want as big of a head start as I can get.

Inching, inching, inching, I'm amazed he doesn't realize what I'm doing. Inching more, drinking water, inching more, drinking water, and perhaps best of all, feeling smarter, better, superior to my opponent. It is the fuel that feeds me like none other. What is this but a contest? A competition to be won or lost? A competition I am going to win.

There, a crack of a twig. Glancing back again, jockey-style, through my armpit, I see he's putting himself away.

Now.

I spring forward and am in full stride before he even moves.

Instead of heading for the driveway, I speed toward thickets of mountain laurel. Being small can be an advantage. I'm hoping the tangle of limbs will let me slide past and hold him back.

Behind me he charges, a thundering rhinoceros.

Into the woods now. Branches and twigs and leaves and even thorns don't seem to touch me. Or maybe I just can't feel them. Everything I am reads the terrain ahead. Left, right, duck, jump, racing and maneuvering and pushing my body to its limits. After only a handful of minutes, I register the fact that the crashing behind me has stopped.

He's gone to get his gun.

I don't slow down.

I stopped running a long time ago. The sun was on its way down when I started, and now it's about four hours closer to the horizon. I do my best to keep it in front of me. Heading due west seems smart. It's the easiest direction to follow, headed straight toward the sun, with the cabin at my back. Just as importantly, going west lets me go more downhill than uphill.

The hills here never stop. It's up and down and up and down and up and down. I stick to the ravines as much as possible, taking cover in the folds of the mountains. The ravines are a mixture of soft, boggy ground and rocks. My feet took some serious hits in my race away from the cabin, so I pick my way along the mushy spots. Along with the soft ground and the cover, I'm hoping the ravines take me down to a river, and that river will take me down to a real road. So far it's nothing but deep wilderness.

Wolfman hasn't shown himself, but I know he's out there. I can't see him or hear him, but I can feel him. It's good news for me that he's working with a .45 handgun. He's going to have to get close to kill me. I'm not a huge fan of guns, but Caleb and Grandpapa have both tried to teach me about them. Some of it sank in. Not much, but some.

The good news is, just about every other ravine has a clear, little stream waterfalling its way down it. The bad news is, I'm dizzy with hunger.

There's no food here. No berries, no nuts. I ate a worm I found, but that's it.

Food. It's taken over my every thought. *Food. Food. Food.*

I'm not used to autumn being so cold, but then I'm not used to being in the mountains, naked. How long can I survive out here? Especially after the sun sets and the cold creeps in? Panic seeps into me, but I recite my goals and feel stronger for it. Only a few minutes later the worry returns. Anxiety and stress are no friends of mine right now. They burn extra calories. Confidence is what I need.

I stop midway down a ravine. For no reason a sense of well-being comes over me.

Something good just happened.

I've never had a psychic experience before, and I wonder if that's what this is. It's not a thought so much as a feeling. It's related to Caleb. Even though I have absolutely no evidence to suggest it, I believe Caleb has figured out something important. He's called me too many times without me answering. He's getting suspicious. He's calling Becca, calling Mom and Dad. He already believes something's wrong. Now he's figuring out what.

It might be just the hunger talking, maybe a hallucination brought on by low blood sugar, but I choose to believe it's real. I choose to let it give me strength and hope.

Coming on toward dusk and I haven't lost faith in my epiphany, but my steps are dragging now. I'm hurting. I'm hurting bad. I can't think. I need food.

The moment the sun dips behind the hills I can feel the temperature drop.

My current ravine broadens into a little meadow. I come around a bend, and the meadow expands into a wide-open field. There's a big oak in the center, and beneath that big oak there is a wooden tub.

I know exactly what that wooden tub is. It's bear bait. It's illegal and a practice I hate. Hunters put out a pile of apples. Bears can't resist it, and it lures them into the open, right into the hunter's trap. But I'm thrilled this hunter has put out his illegal bear bait.

Jogging toward the tub, I try not to get too hopeful. Maybe there won't be any apples. But even then, maybe there's a hunting cabin nearby. Maybe I'm getting close to civilization. But mostly I'm just hoping for food.

Collapsing next to the tub, I peer inside and see them. Dozens and dozens of apples. They're not even rotten. Soft, but not rotten. The first one goes down in a second. The second one takes no longer. Never in my life has anything tasted as good as these apples. They're manna from heaven.

My head is buried in the tub when I hear it.

A high-powered-rifle shot.

I sit up tall, like a deer listening for danger.

Everything inside me stops, and for a split second I live in denial. *They're hunting bear. It's not for you.*

That denial is destroyed by a bullet. It slides past my left shoulder, a grazing shot that slices my deltoid as elegantly as a scalpel. It is blood and burning and numbness from the shoulder down, but adrenaline hides the pain.

I run in pure animal panic.

A third bullet chases my heels, but misses. I dive into the ravines. They give me cover, and the gunshots stop. He must be on a ridge. Still running, I glance up along the ridgeline. There's nothing to see but trees.

Stupidly, my first thought is that this isn't fair. I didn't know he had a hunting rifle. I never saw it. I only saw the handgun. I didn't know what I was up against. It's not fair. None of this is fair.

"Life isn't fair," comes the voice of Nana. She has told me that a thousand times. "What matters is how you handle it."

I'm going to handle it by winning.

The sun has hidden itself behind the hills, and in the gloaming my pale skin shines white in the darkness. I might as well have drawn a target on myself.

Victory is in the details.

I should have known better.

Coming upon a boggy spot, I flop down into the mud and roll, roll, roll, until I'm black and green and brown all over. Above me is a rocky outcropping, covered by a downed tree. I slip my way between the rock and the tree, my back against the hillside.

Time to pause and listen. And there it is. The sound of footsteps crawls into my heart and my lungs, making it hard to breathe, hard to pump blood through my body.

Leaning my head back, I stare at the ridge above me.

There he is, silhouetted against what's left of the daylight. He is a big, black shape, and in his hands I see the sleek outline of a hunting rifle, a powerful scope perched atop it.

He is coming for me.

I am naked, without a weapon.

My one good arm is now wounded.

I have paid dearly for my meal.

Forty Years Ago

THE SMALL CABIN IS IMMACULATE IN THE WAY ONLY something brand-new can be. The boy, a fifteen-year-old who looks eighteen, sits at attention, happily craning his neck to take in all the details of the place. At his feet are two splotchy-colored hunting dogs. He pets one and then the other, scratching them behind the ears. His uncle Lou is giving him a long-winded spiel about how he built the cabin with his own two hands. Most would find it boring at best, but not the boy. To him this is something close to heaven.

His uncle pauses, and the boy focuses in on the older man. They look like they could be father and son, instead of just uncle and nephew. The boy senses something important is about to be said.

"I want you to have this cabin after I'm gone, Jerry."

"What?"

"You heard me. I want it to stay in the family, with blood. I suppose

Jenny or Marleen could inherit it, but what use would they get out of it? Maybe if they get married, their husbands would come up here, but I don't want no damn son-in-law having this place. No, when I die, I want you to have it. Already talked to my lawyer, had it added to my will."

"Uncle Lou, I don't know what to say."

"You just say thank you."

"Thank you."

"You're welcome. And don't think I haven't been watching you. Ever since we came up, you've been looking around like a kid in a candy store. I think you might love this place as much as I do."

It's too much for the boy to wrap his mind around, so he just nods emphatically.

"And like I've said, I've been watching you." Uncle Lou pauses, then says in a low voice, "I see the bruises are still coming."

The boy's happiness evaporates.

"It's nothing to be ashamed of, son. It's not your fault. It's your daddy's fault for leaving y'all behind when you were nothing but a june bug in the bassinet. Jerry, you know what a man's job is?"

"No."

"The job of the man is to keep the woman in line. It's his job to be boss, keep things clear and orderly. If a man doesn't run a tight ship, you get things like the way Avanelle is now. Don't get me wrong; when she was young, she was just as bad. Difference was, Daddy whupped her proper and that kept her managed. Once your daddy run off, and Avanelle was head of her own household, she was allowed to run amuck. So those bruises aren't your fault, Jerry. They're your daddy's fault. He's the one who should be ashamed."

The boy looks pensive. Uncle Lou seems to read his mind. "It's Avanelle's fault too. But women, generally speaking, will run amuck without a man to be the boss. So try not to be too hard on your mama, Jerry. She's just a woman."

He nods, but he doesn't look particularly convinced.

"Now, I'm going to take a little nap. Why don't you do some hog scouting? You can take Boy and Biscuit with you, if you want."

Two hours later the boy returns with the dogs. Happy once more, breathless from exercise, he gives his report.

"Went down by the bear bucket and over two klicks northeast to Ravine B and found a sow, but she had piglets, so . . ." The boy's sentence trails off into nothing. He sits down, knowing there will be no hunting today. Boy and Biscuit put their chins on his knees, and he playfully pushes them away. Tails start to wag and a game develops.

Behind the boy, Uncle Lou straps himself down with two massive hunting knives and a rifle. "Don't know why you're getting comfortable."

There is disapproval in the man, disapproval that sends an electric shock down the boy's spine. He jumps to his feet and grabs his coat.

"Let's go get us a pig," says Uncle Lou.

The boy isn't sure if he's referring to the sow, because that doesn't seem right, or finding a different hog altogether. Either way, he's not going to say a word.

He washes his hands in the cold creek. They're shaking. The sleeves of his coat are soaked in blood.

"Don't you forget the knife," Uncle Lou says.

The boy picks up the hunting knife and lets the water wash away the red. Along the gravelly bank is a line of dead piglets.

Uncle Lou stands over him. Watching him. Bearing down into him.

Biscuit limps up. Before the hog died, she did her work on the hound. The dog laps water from the creek, holding one forepaw in the air all the while.

The boy can feel what's coming before it comes, so he closes his eyes tight, but he can't close his ears, and the rifle shot is deafening. His eyes are still shut, closing him into blackness, when his uncle says, "You can't be afraid of killing."

CHAPTER SIX

I'M STRUCK BY HOW SLOWLY HE WALKS. HE'S TAKING HIS time. There's no urgency, no panic, no worry in him. He's confident. Maybe even enjoying himself, taking in the whole experience. It seems so impossible that a human could be this inhuman.

As I sink even deeper into the rocky hillside, my fingers touch something warm and sticky. It's my own blood, flowing from the bullet wound. I don't feel real pain, only a vague hum of burning numbness.

He's getting closer.

It occurs to me he also walks slowly because he doesn't want to miss a thing. He's being careful. Despite all of his earlier sloppiness, not tying me to the couch and going gunless during the hose-down, I now feel an attention to detail. Out here, hunting in the wilderness, Wolfman is in his element.

And it terrifies me.

Now, more than ever, he has the upper hand. He holds all the cards. Against the rocks, naked and injured, I have no advantages.

He disappears from view, but I can hear him. After a few minutes, his footsteps grow louder again.

He's sweeping the hillside. Back and forth, back and forth. Searching out all the crevices.

What can I do? How can I win this? A terrible conclusion begins to feel inevitable. But I want to win. Not only for me, but for Mom and Dad and Grandpapa and Nana. For Caleb. I want to make them proud of me. But I can't win this. There's no way I can run. He's far too close, and his gun is too powerful. I don't think I can sneak away and stay quiet enough. In the silence of the autumn forest I can hear every sound he's making. My own movement would be just as obvious.

I half close my eyes, worried the whites of them might give me away.

Staring at the forest, I wonder if this is the last thing I will ever see.

Is this how the girls felt before they died? Did they feel the noose of inevitability tightening around their necks? Did they give up? I hope they fought. That they never gave up. That they never gave him that satisfaction.

Be here for me, I pray to them. *Be here for me and make me strong.* I then think: *Help me. If you can help me, help me now.*

Something comes into focus. I am looking at a deer. A buck with an enormous rack of antlers. He stands, still as a statue, many yards away. It is only thanks to a perfect window through many bushes and trees that I can see him at all.

It seems he looks at me, just as I look at him.

He is beautiful.

Run, I think. *Run as fast as you can. Make him think you're me.*

But he stands, seemingly fearless, unstartled by me, unstartled by the presence of the Wolfman.

Run! You are in danger! Run!

I scream so loud inside my own skull I almost drown out the sound of the Wolfman's steps. They are so close, too close—they're on top of me.

Help me.

Wolfman takes a bad step. A rock crashes down the ravine.

The stag runs.

He is big and he is loud, but thanks to the undergrowth, he is invisible. Wolfman takes off after him. He's no longer slow and careful; now he's excited by the hunt.

Thank you. Thank you. Thank you.

Quiet returns to the forest. He is gone. For now.

Exhaustion comes over me, and there, clinging to my rocks, I fall out of consciousness and into a dream. But this time I do not know I'm dreaming, and it's not a memory dream. It's more hallucination than anything.

In my dream the other redheaded girls come to me. There are six of them. They do not say a word, but they surround me as I lie in the ravine. They want to help and comfort me.

I look into their faces. They're all younger than me, twelve to fifteen years old, maybe. Some still have cheeks that carry the soft roundness of childhood.

"What are your names?" I ask, but they say nothing.

"How old are you?" I try again.

Finally I say, "Does anyone know what happened to you?"

One girl makes eye contact and shakes her head no. She has dark eyes, and her hair is so deeply red it's almost brown. There is so much sorrow radiating from her it makes me want to cry.

For the first time I consider what would happen to my family and friends if I just disappeared and never came back. How would they deal with not knowing? Would it be better than knowing my fate? No, I'd rather they know. If for no other reason than that they would bring this man to justice.

Which is one more reason why I can't fail. It's *my* job. That fight would be too much for them. I need to do this.

My eyes water. The Wolfman tried to take my family away from me with his notebook and mind games, but I know they love me. And I love them.

The girls huddle around me now, tucking my muddy hair behind my ears, wiping my tears away, softly touching my wounds and making them feel better. Their expressions are somber, strong, compassionate. They are here for me, and they understand.

I think: *I am not alone.*

And wake up.

The moon is still low in the sky; the mud is still wet on my skin. My wounds feel the same as they ever did. Not much has changed. But I feel better for having had my dream-hallucination about the other redheaded girls; I feel stronger, more able to think.

What do I do now?

My first thought is to continue heading west, away from the cabin. It's natural instinct kicking in; it's what makes sense to the part of me controlled by fear.

But that's not who I am. I win by taking risks. By standing out. Mom hates how I ride Tucker right past the judge as many times as possible in a class. She says it's showboating and it's tacky. Some judges don't like it. Long ago, though, I decided I'd rather win being me than lose by playing it safe.

So what would the classic Ruth Ann Carver move be? What would he not expect?

Well, I think, *I could steal his truck.*

Five Years Ago

IT'S HARD NOT TO FEEL SMALL, TAKING IN THE WARM-UP ring. The most famous trainers riding the most valuable quarter horses are crammed in there, fighting for practice space.

"I'll be in this corner, okay?" her mother says.

The girl nods obediently, with no intention of actually obeying. She hopes it looks like it's the traffic that forces her to pick a spot in the opposite corner from where her mother is stationed.

A competitor since age three, she doesn't consider herself young and inexperienced. She feels she is a grizzled veteran of a thousand wars. Which is why she hasn't let herself get too excited about the last two weeks, despite the glimpses of greatness her horse has given her. That was at home. Here, in the chaos of the Oklahoma City Fairgrounds, it may be a different story.

She jogs her black gelding along the rail, letting his muscles come to life. Their routine is burned into her brain. Circles left, circles right, transitions from walk to jog to lope, then pushing him into an extended lope, his long strides eating up the ground like he's hungry for dirt. Halt, back, side pass. Only a few times does she ask him for show-off moves, sliding stops and rollbacks and spins. No point in drilling a skill that's already solid.

With every movement, her horse is with her. More than with her, he is a part of her. All that is required is a thought, and then that thought comes to life in the form of perfect motion. She knows it's her nervous system carrying those thoughts through her body, creating tiny movements her horse is reading. Knowing this doesn't make it any less magic. Her horse is happy and she is happy and this is the one place in all the world where everything makes sense, everything is as it should be. She is in perfect control, and it is so pleasing to her, that sense of control, that sense of power.

Satisfied with the practice, she asks her horse to halt. She gives him a pat and murmurs words of praise. Her focus released, she is now free to absorb what is around her, truly and completely. There is conflict. Conflict everywhere. Trainers riding horses too roughly. Trainers yelling at their clients. Horses pinning their ears in anger. It's all wrong. Suffocatingly wrong. She's seen plenty of bad riding in her life, but she thought here, at Worlds, it would be different. Instead, she is the one who is different from the rest. A sensation of disconnect and inadequacy weighs her down.

The girl looks to the corner, to her mother, who gives her a double thumbs-up. She feels a swell of gratitude. Her mother may not bring in the big-money clients, but she's a real horsewoman. Her mother has taught her right. The girl is proud she rides the way she does. It's occurred to her before that this is what should be rewarded at horse shows, that her mother's methods deserve recognition. Now the old thought comes home with new force.

She takes in the same scene—the yelling trainers, the unhappy horses—but now a beautiful thought comes shining through.

I am better than them.

The girl pilots her horse out of the arena to where her mother is waiting, a giant smile on her face. Guilt stings the girl. She shouldn't have hidden from her mom the way she did.

"That was so good!"

"Thanks, Mom." She mumbles the words, ashamed.

"And it was smart of you to find your own space away from me. That's thinking like a competitor. You needed your own quiet area to work in and you made it happen. That's exactly how I want you to think, because that's how you become a winner."

Her chest expands; her spine straightens. "Really?"

"Yes, really. Winners are ruthless, Ruth. Ha, that's funny. Anyway, point is, in order to be a winner you have to be tough and not worry about other people's feelings. I'm proud of you for being more concerned about getting in a good practice than you were about what I had to say."

"Huh," she says, letting the unexpected words seep into her bones.

CHAPTER SEVEN

MY HOPE IS TO REACH THE CABIN BY DAWN, BUT I HAVE no idea if that's possible. I'm colder than I think is good for me. Sometimes half an idea flirts around the edges of my thinking.

I should be in more pain.

But whenever it pops up, I push it away, worried if the idea gets too much attention the pain will come to the surface. My feet are chewed up; both arms are injured. There's been too much blood lost from the cut on my head and the bullet slice to the arm. Only two and a half apples have made their way into my stomach.

But at least I'm hydrated.

That's huge.

And maybe why I seem to be thinking pretty well.

The deer bolted in a westerly direction, leading Wolfman

further west. Of course he won't find me there, and at a certain point he will give up and go back to the cabin.

The odds are against me. I know that. Wolfman knows these woods; I don't. The chances that I can do anything like retrace my steps are low to nil. I've had a feeling that civilization would be found by going down in elevation, by going west. But that's nothing but a feeling. I could just as easily run into a hunting cabin going east.

If I can just get to the truck, it would be game over.

And it would be such a satisfying way to win, too. To take something of his out from under his nose. I imagine him returning to the cabin to find the truck missing. Would he feel fear? Apprehension? Even if he did, he wouldn't feel even 1 percent of the terror he's put into others. But I'll take what I can get.

Thinking back to the last time I was in the cabin, I can't remember if I saw the keys hanging on the nail by the door. But those keys weren't in his pants pockets, of that I'm pretty sure, and that's what's important. Those keys are somewhere in that cabin.

As I make my way, I take in everything. Searching for landmarks and sometimes finding them. *This dead oak. I remember this dead oak!* And looking for signs of either myself or Wolfman. *My footprint, in a bit of sand. I'm headed the right way.*

It's slow going, and time and time again things look wrong and I retrace and start over. I need patience now, but patience is something I have. When you're starting a young horse, you've sometimes got to go at a glacial pace. Practicing a new skill takes repetition, repetition, and more repetition. This is something I know how to do. I know how to work a problem.

Frustration is the enemy. It makes you do stupid things. So you don't let it beat you. Instead you search for landmarks, look for signs, search for landmarks, look for signs. The task takes every single bit of me I have left.

It's good, this task, because it keeps my mind focused.

Things are going well. But then moonlight gives way to predawn gray. I don't like that. My gut tells me he'll go back to the cabin once morning hits. For food, if nothing else.

I don't want to be at that cabin at the same time he's there. Then I smile and think, *The understatement of the year.*

This goal of stealing the truck has been good for me. A little bit of my personality is surfacing. It's strange when I see it, like an old friend I'd completely forgotten.

I keep working the problem. Searching for landmarks, looking for signs.

In the background I recite my goals, with my new, fourth goal: *Steal his truck and ride to victory.* Between reciting goals, I think of the other girls, and of my family and friends, and I ask them for their prayers, their energy, their good intentions. These thoughts help.

The sun comes up in earnest, but I won't let worry and frustration take over.

I don't know where I am, but I feel like I should be there by now. The sun has been up for a while. A long while. Wolfman will want to eat breakfast. Or is it lunch? When did he head back to the cabin? Is he already there?

There hasn't been a landmark in a long time.

Pretty soon it'll be time to give up.

The thought scares me, but in the end, what's the difference between lost in a westerly direction and lost in an easterly direction? Either way, the important thing is to find help. Find a hunting cabin or a road.

Even though I tell myself this, it feels like defeat. With the disappointment my energy ebbs. The quest for the truck kept me going. It gave me a goal. Without that goal, I have nothing.

Get it together, Ruthie.

Maybe I won't get to steal his truck. So what? The idea had a lot of appeal, but in truth how much of that was just me wanting to show off? Besides, is the risk really worth the reward? Probably not. Getting the keys, getting to the truck, getting out of there—all of that is extremely high risk. What if the keys aren't on the nail? What if he grabs me before I get to the truck? What if the truck won't start and then he grabs me?

Not finding the cabin, not finding the truck, this is all a blessing. I need to accept it as such and move on with a new plan.

Just then I turn my head to the left, and there it is.

The truck.

Parked out front of the cabin.

Somehow I circled around the cabin, got in front of it, and damn near wandered to the front door.

Dear God, I'm an idiot. An idiot, an idiot, an idiot.

I find a hole to hide in. Some time ago a big, old oak fell over, and its pulled-up roots left a nice, me-size hole in the earth. I clamber into it, feeling a little safer as I get my wits together. I had no clue how close I was to the cabin. No clue. The thought leaves me shaky.

Time to steady my breathing, steady my hands. Think. Time to think.

The good news is, I don't see or hear anything. If I'm lucky, he's far out west, hunting for me. But that's no certainty, and my blundering path through the woods has shaken my confidence.

Does it make such a difference, though, whether I approach the cabin from the back or the front? Isn't the important thing that I'm here now, twenty yards from the truck?

On the other hand, I'd made some good arguments. Going to get the keys, that's just crazy. Out in the forest it sounded like a great idea. To me, squatting here in this hole in the ground, naked except for mud and blood, it sounds insane. Why would I go back into that cabin?

My mind pings back and forth, fear telling me to run and abandon my plan, courage telling me to stick it out. In the end, what decides it is the sight of my own body, the soles of my feet. I'm in terrible shape. I need out of this godforsaken wilderness.

The reward outweighs the risk.

No longer motivated by the idea of his shock and fear, no longer motivated by anything other than the desire to get this over with, I advance toward the house.

It's a hum. Everything is a hum. Sights, sounds, sensation, it all melds into a hum around me. I want to keep sharp, but I'm dulled by fear. I'm stuffed full of it.

There are only a few trees between me and the front door now.

It's now or never.

Before I'm really ready, I run.

Please, please, don't be home, don't be home.

Reaching the front door, I sling open the barricade, throw open the door, and find the keys on the nail. Like they were waiting for me.

I grab them.

Time does funny things, and now I'm in the truck without any memory of how I got there. I turn the key, and the old engine cranks.

"Oh, good truck, good truck," I say.

I floor it.

This old truck has power. More power than I'm used to.

And now I know why he was so slow, so careful on this path that doesn't even count for a road. The curves and bumps send me to two wheels.

I'm going to crash before I've even gone a quarter of a mile.

I release the gas, and the truck returns to all fours, but it's jouncing up and down like I'm in an inflatable bouncy castle. No seat belt on, I can't quite get a good grip on the wheel. There's a bend in the road; I manage to crank right and follow the clearing.

And there he is.

Right in front of me.

With every bit of strength I have, I punch the gas pedal hard. Hard, hard, hard. I want to crash into him; I want to kill him; I want to flatten him.

The truck bears down on the Wolfman.

He half raises his gun, and I think, *Yes, mother-effer, take the time to raise your gun; take your time and see what it gets you.*

But he's too smart. He abandons the gun, letting it sling useless against his side, and leaps into the brush as the truck barrels past.

He's behind me now, but I'm still not in control. It's too fast; everything's too fast. Another sharp bend almost sends me into a tree. Hitting the brake hard, I then try to figure out a pace that's doable on this treacherous mountain lane.

Sticking with the pace for a few seconds, I think of Wolfman gaining ground, climbing a ridge. Once he's on a ridge, with that hunting rifle, he'll look through his scope and he'll see me. He'll shoot up the truck. He'll get me. He can still get me. I know he can still get me.

I want to stop myself, but I can't. My right foot can't stop pushing the gas pedal, sending the truck lurching down the path. The road forks. I choose left.

Only two hundred yards later I hit a dead end.

It takes a million-point turn before I can get the truck going back to where I came from.

I'm ready to see him, standing in the lane, his rifle at the ready.

He's not there, not in person, but he's in my mind. He looms so large I can't get away from him. I get back to the fork and go the other way. Just a few seconds later and I'm forced to face another choice.

I don't want these damn choices; I want a route out. I want out of here.

But there is no clear path. There's a labyrinth of country roads, more trails than roads, really, and I don't know where the hell I am.

I pick a road, but in no time I face another dead end.

And another.

And now I have no idea where I am.

I take yet another path that ends in a dead end, and I recognize it as a dead end I've already visited. I'm driving in circles. I'm not getting out.

I'd thought this truck was my trip to victory. Now I hate it. I hate it like I've never hated an inanimate object in my life. I hate the way it lurches; I hate the rotten mildew smell of it. It can't get me where I want to go. It can't get me anywhere but lost. Inside it I'm big and loud and visible; I'm an easy target.

These poor excuses for roads follow the low spots, the valleys. I'm a slow-moving bug down in a rut, and the Wolfman is up there somewhere, up on the ridges, with his high-powered rifle and his scope, and he's waiting for me.

How long have I been driving? I don't know, but I'm covered with sweat.

I've focused my energies, picking my way forward, making mental landmarks of where I've been. It's impossible to say if I'm taking the best path possible, but at least I'm not making the same dead-end mistakes over and over again. It takes a while, far longer than I'd like, but I find myself on a well-maintained gravel road. It's a huge improvement over the trails and dirt lanes of the morning. It's a strange road though. The gravel is piled on inches thick, and it's broader than you'd expect.

Driving conservatively, driving to preserve every drop of gas in the tank, I follow the gravel road like it's a lifeline. Because it is.

It goes on and on and on and on and on and on, and I start to worry about how much gas I have left. It dawns on me that this is a DNR road. Department of Natural Resources. It's kept up not because people are ever on it. It's kept up in case of wildfire or other natural disaster. All the same, even a DNR road will meet up with a real road eventually. I've started to lose faith in miracles, but one might happen, and I might run into a forest ranger making his patrols.

Up ahead there's something long and solid and white gray. It stretches across the road, and the sight of it puts a lead weight of dread into my belly. I think I know what it is, but I hope I'm wrong. Or maybe there's a way around it I just can't see yet.

With every yard it becomes clearer, and soon there's no hope, no denying what it is.

A concrete barricade. There's no way around it. No road beyond it.

This "road" I'm on is nothing but a firebreak. It's not a road at all.

When I'm finally turned back to the direction I came from, the fuel light blinks on.

It's too much.

The engine is loud, and when I pull the key out of the ignition, the silence is like a vacuum. I need to take a break, think.

But I don't think.

I feel.

I feel rage and hate, self-pity and sorrow; I feel soul-scorching waves of agony. I want to punch my way out of reality and into a different world, but instead I hit the steering wheel, because it's right there. I hit it as hard as I can, until I can hit no more.

And then words come, words to no one in particular, except to God, who I know can hear me.

"I need out!" I bellow, like a cow being slaughtered. I bellow again. "I need out; get me out of here, now!"

Nothing happens. Nothing comes to whisk me away. No guardian angels, no Good Samaritans. No one comes for me. I am alone. Completely alone.

I hit the steering wheel one more time.

"Please let me out!"

I have been forsaken.

Thirty-Seven Years Ago

IN THE LIBRARY THE YOUNG MAN HOVERS OVER A CLUSTER of open books. Next to him is a girl his own age, but she looks a lot younger. She is delicate, small, with black hair, dark brown eyes, and olive skin. Although she is quite pretty, there is a bookishness about her that hides her looks. The young man is eighteen but could pass for thirty. He is big and broad and has a five-o'clock shadow.

His eyes travel over the girl next to him, coveting her. She doesn't seem to mind the attention.

She points out a line in a reference book. "This is good. We can use this."

He writes down the quote and where it came from with enthusiasm. "This is more than good. It's perfect. Boy howdy, this project is going to save my grade."

The girl studies him as he diligently records the citation. She says, "It's nice when you talk, you know. You're always so quiet in class."

He turns a few different colors, at a complete loss for words.

"Why don't you ever talk in class?"

"Most people aren't nice. Like you."

It is her turn to change shades, but her tan cheeks give her camouflage. They both return to the books in self-conscious silence. His mouth works nervously. He has something he wants to say, but hardly the courage to say it. The girl sees his struggle.

"What?" she asks.

"I was wondering if you'd want to go to prom with me?"

He can see it's not an automatic no. Hope rises in the boy.

"But that's this weekend. I don't have a dress or anything."

"Wear that. I don't care."

He grins; she grins back.

"I couldn't wear this! That would be ridiculous." But she's still grinning; she's considering it.

"It would be fun. Afterwards I could take you up to my cabin."

"What?" There's a shift in her. Not a good shift. His eagerness blinds him to the change.

"Yeah, I have my own cabin. It belongs to me."

"How do you have a cabin?"

"I inherited it. When my uncle died."

"How did he die?" She shifts further away from him, but he doesn't feel it.

"Hunting accident. But don't worry about that; it's a great cabin. Up in the Blue Ridge. It's so pretty up there, you'd love it."

"In the Blue Ridge? Jerry, that's got to be a two-hour drive, at least."

"I ride up there all the time; it's no big deal. C'mon, really. You should come with me."

"No, there's no way my parents would be okay with that. Let's just get back to work, okay?" She turns her body away from his, her gaze on the pages before her.

He doesn't return to studying. He sits, motionless, watching her.

She senses the silence. "Let's get back to work," she says. She's about to say something else, but the words leave her when she looks into his eyes. The moment lasts far too long. The boy observes her expression travel from irritation to confusion to understanding and finally to fear. She has seen into him.

He always knew she was smart, but he didn't realize just how smart she was. From now on, the boy knows, she will be on guard with him. She will never be alone with him. She will protect herself from what she saw. He wants to tell her there isn't anything for her *to be afraid of; she's different, special. But maybe she's not. Maybe she's right to be scared.*

CHAPTER EIGHT

FOR SOME TIME I SIT BEHIND THE WHEEL, HATING THE truck beyond all reason, trying to will a new reality into being. No matter how hard I curse the truck, or God, or how hard I try to will something new into existence, nothing changes. The old Chevy truck stays the same. The road stays the same. And I stay stuck.

My hate doesn't leave me, but I choose to leave this place. The fact I'm driving straight back to the Wolfman's lair is not lost on me. He's up in those ridges, waiting. Perhaps he knew where I was going before I did; maybe he's resting, knowing I'd be back. Possibly he knows exactly where I'll emerge from this firebreak lane.

As I drive, I try to think about my friends and family, about Caleb, about the other girls before me, but then I see the gas light glowing, I see how low the sun is in the sky, and rage kills these thoughts.

All I have now is rage.

But somewhere, hiding underneath it, is fear.

The fear is like a roller coaster, *click, click, click*ing upward as I drive toward him. My thick layer of camo mud has sloughed off, leaving a filthy residue. Underneath the dirt, my skin has broken out in hives.

I drive and drive and drive.

I'm amazed I haven't run out of gas.

Possibly the truck is fueled by my rage and fear. That's a renewable resource.

Finally a dirt lane comes into view. I get off the firebreak and head back into the maze, doing my best to avoid old mistakes, sticking strictly to new ones. Either way, I'm driving around the Wolfman's backyard, and it's as though the very air is filled with his stink. He's everywhere around me, inescapable.

I can't stop craning my neck, checking out the ridgelines. He's up there somewhere; there's no question. But the cover is too thick. I can't see him, but I also can't fight the compulsion to look, even though it's only adding to my anxiety.

The sun is about to set. Night will remove all hope of spotting him.

Yet another hairpin turn takes me to a new part of the valley. This is good. I definitely haven't been here before. Maybe I'm making my way out. Any bit of optimism makes me paranoid, and I immediately check the hilltops, looking for Wolfman.

That's when I see it.

A house on a hill.

There aren't any lights on, but even if it's empty, it's shelter.

Maybe food. Clothes. Possibly even a weapon. I head for it, like a beacon. Other forks in the road present themselves, but it's easy to make decisions now. I just keep heading for the house on the hill.

The sun drops below the horizon, and a miracle occurs. Lights turn on in the house on the hill. Somebody's home. Somebody is there. The closer I get, the worse I feel. I'm almost saved now, and as my adrenaline unclenches its iron fist on my body, every one of my injuries comes screaming to life.

My scalp, my right arm, my bullet wound, my feet. This is what I've been afraid of. I knew the pain was there, real and alive and just under the surface, waiting to get out, waiting for my mind to give up and set it free. The sight of the house has set all of my nerves free to scream.

The truck sputters to a halt. It's out of gas.

I don't know how I'll climb the steep driveway to the front door.

Lowering myself carefully to the ground, I see a portable gas tank stuck behind the bench seat. I shake it and find it's full. Gasoline was never a problem; it was just a problem I hadn't fully investigated.

I consider filling the tank so I can drive the final twenty yards, but the idea exhausts me. It seems easier to make the walk.

Up on this vantage point, I get a sense of just how short the distance I've traveled really is. Down below me is a squiggling valley, offering hairpin turn after hairpin turn. That is where I spent my day, lost. On this hill, though, I can see the shortcuts, the ridgelines that connect peak to peak to peak. That is where Wolfman probably spent his day, knowing exactly where he was.

An uptick of fear puts my painful body into motion. It hurts to move, but there's still enough adrenaline to get me to the finish line.

I stay focused on the house. It's a beautiful log cabin, new and expensive. It looks like a place my parents would rent for a family weekend.

These twenty yards are killing me, but then I hear movement inside. Hope spurs me on, as does relief. This is all about to be over. I'm about to be rescued. I'm about to win.

Climbing the porch steps takes everything I have. The front door is inset with a complicated pattern of beveled glass, and I can see warped fragments of the luxurious interior. Heart-of-pine floors, leather sofa. It's clean and neat and pretty.

I can also see shadows of my reflection in the glass door. It's only a hint of my appearance, but I avoid even that. It's too disturbing.

Now that I'm at the front door, I can smell food. Their dinner. My mouth waters as I knock on the beveled glass. Meat and corn on the cob. I'm salivating so much I have to swallow my own spit.

Next to the front door is a wooden sign that says THE LOGAN FAMILY LODGE.

A silver-haired man appears in the hallway. He stands stock-still and stares at me.

I knock again.

A woman joins the man. She's older, too, but her hair is dyed dark. They look like models from a Lands' End catalogue.

I knock a third time.

The silver-haired man barks at his wife. "Get back! It's a naked girl!"

She disappears around the corner, and I realize this isn't going to go as I imagined.

Knocking, I yell, "I need help!"

"Get away from here!" he yells back.

"I've been attacked. I've been kidnapped. I need help." I want to sound calm, but I don't even get close to calm. Even to my own ears I sound like a wild animal.

The wife says something from her hidey-hole. The man turns his head and says, "Honey, it's one of these meth addicts. They'll do anything."

"I'm not a meth addict. I've been kidnapped. My name is Ruth Carver. Please, you've got to help me."

"Whoever you are, I'm giving you until the count of three."

My ability to stay calm completely shot, I scream at him, "Please call 911! Tell them you have Ruth Carver at your house!"

"You need to leave right this second."

Again the woman says something I can't hear from around the corner.

"You're right," the man says. "Maybe it's some kind of trap."

My pain disappears. Not out of fear this time, but out of angry disbelief. "A trap? *A trap?* How in the hell is calling 911 ever going to be a trap? God, you idiot! You stupid idiot!"

He stands there, silent.

"Please, call 911 and tell them you have a meth addict attacking your house!"

"You need to leave *now.*"

"Let me talk to your wife, please." My hope is I can get her to understand. She is a woman. She has to understand.

"You're not talking to my wife."

I yell loudly, so she can hear me. "Mrs. Logan, please come talk to me!" I hear nothing. "Please! Please just listen to what I have to say. That can't hurt you."

Mrs. Logan edges out from around the corner. I press my hands and face against her expensive beveled-glass door, hoping she'll be able to look into my eyes and see I'm telling the truth.

"Mrs. Logan, my name is Ruth Carver. I'm seventeen years old. I live in Mauldin, South Carolina, with a nice family. I have no idea where I am right now. I've been taken by a man named Jerry Balls. He was a man my dad hired a year ago. Mrs. Logan, this man is a rapist. He is a murderer. And he is after me. He is after me, Mrs. Logan."

The woman takes small steps toward me. I think she wants to get a better look at my face, see if I'm honest.

"You have to believe me, because I'm telling the truth. This man is out here, right now, in these woods, and he is after me. He is going to rape and kill me." I find myself fighting back emotion, which only makes me angrier. "Please believe me."

She turns toward her husband. They look into each other's eyes. I can't tell what's happening; all I know is that this is taking too long. More and more, I'm feeling the darkness of the night at my back. I'm standing up against a lit window like a moth, the Wolfman's truck is out front, and I'm a sitting duck for a long-range hunting rifle.

I hit my fists against the glass. "Please, let me in! He's out here with me!"

Finally Mrs. Logan speaks. "I believe her."

Sinking to my knees in relief, I wait for them to come open the door.

The woman adds, "We have to get her out of here."

Crumpling into a ball, I'm close to weeping.

"Get her out of here!" the woman says.

It takes several seconds for me to understand the meaning of her words. It's like she's speaking in a foreign language, but the tone cuts through to my heart. Her voice is like steel. There is no mercy in her words, only urgent self-preservation.

All the same, I say, "What? What are you talking about?"

She turns to me and says, "You need to go."

"Are you crazy?"

"Go. Get out of here."

It's too much. That this person—that this *woman*—believes me and still won't help is too much for me to take. I'm not scared of them, and whether they like it or not, they'll have to deal with me on the other side of the door.

"I am not going to die out here!" I grab the doorknob with both hands and turn.

The husband disappears.

I expected the door to be unlocked, to swing open, but it doesn't. I fight with it, as though it's just stuck and not locked and dead bolted. Breathing hard, I give up on the door, but not on my cause. Looking Mrs. Logan in the eye, I sit down in protest.

"I'm not leaving until you call 911. I'm staying right here until you call them." We stare at one another, and I find myself hating her almost as much as I hate the Wolfman.

"You need to leave."

"I swear to God, I am going to sue the ever-living fuck out of you once this is all over."

She says nothing, her eyes ice cold.

I believe mine are even colder. "Every person I meet for the rest of my life I am going to tell them about you and what you've done tonight."

The meat and corn and potatoes hang heavy in the air. I swallow my spit once more. "Can you at least give me some food?"

She doesn't move, but then I didn't really expect her to.

Swinging around the corner, the man reappears, a handgun in his fist. Crazy-eyed, he marches down the long hallway toward me, looking dangerously incompetent. He holds the weapon like he's scared of it.

"Oh God," I groan. Clambering to my feet, I somehow manage to run away from the front door. Skirting the edge of the house, I duck around to the side, pause, and listen. There is nothing to hear. Mr. Logan didn't even have the courage to open the front door, which doesn't surprise me in the least.

Despite their reluctance to call 911, my guess is that the Logans won't have the guts to leave their house until they get a police escort. When the cops do show up, I want them to find something important.

The side of the house has too many windows, so I sneak

around to the back and find a detached garage. It is nice and white, but it's also in the open. Wolfman's out here. I feel him. But this is something I need to do. Fighting back my fear, I get down to business.

A rotting pinecone seems like a good thing to try, and it works the way I hoped it would. Using the garage door like a piece of paper, I scratch *Ruth Carver taken by Jerry T. Balls,* followed by his address. It takes a total of three pinecones to complete. I can't pull up the zip code, but everything else remains in my memory.

I hear the sound of an engine and tires on gravel. It gives me hope. People live around here. This has to be close to civilization. Now all I need to do is fill up the truck and keep going.

Wary of Mr. Logan's incompetence, I take the long way back to the truck.

At first I think I've become disoriented.

Because I can't find it. I can't find the truck.

But I'm not disoriented. The truck is gone.

It has been taken.

I try to delude myself into thinking Mr. Logan took it, but I look up at the brightly lit house and see both the Logans looking out into the night. They saw the truck drive away and probably didn't have a good enough view to realize I wasn't the driver.

The engine sound I heard earlier wasn't a hopeful sound, after all. It was the sound of a noose tightening around my neck.

Five Years Ago

SHE IS TIRED AND SWEATY AND COVERED WITH DUST AND mud when she sees him.

"Caleb!"

Always quiet, he answers with a grin.

She leaves her horse cross tied in the wash rack and runs toward him. He knows what she's up to and turns tail, sprinting away from her. They make some rich people in a golf cart mad, but they don't care. The chase lasts until the end of the barn aisle, where the girl snatches him up and makes sure she transfers as much filth onto the boy as she can.

Slapping his back in a fake hug, she says, "It's so good to see you!"

He gives in and returns the hug. "It's good to see you, too, Ruthie."

And then the hug isn't a friend's method of good-humored torture. The hug is something else, something that makes the girl feel uncomfortable, and she lets go.

"C'mon," she says. "I don't want Tucker to freak out without me."

"Tucker ain't never freaked out a day in his life," the boy rejoins.

The girl tenses at the use of "ain't." She looks over at him as they walk side by side. As usual, he's wearing those damn Wranglers. The girl almost shakes her head. They're going to a new middle school next year. It was barely acceptable to wear Wranglers at their old school in the country, and the new school is pure suburbia. She tried to talk to him about it once, but he wouldn't listen. Insisted he was who he was and he wasn't going to change for anybody. She feels bad about it, but if he wants to dig his own grave, it's on him.

"What are you looking at?" the boy asks.

"Nothing," she says. "Just glad you're here." Once she says it, it becomes true, and she forgets the Wranglers. No one important is here to see his cowboy jeans anyway. She throws an arm around his neck, back to the game of smearing dirt on him.

They walk out into the sunshine, and the boy pauses for a long look at the Jim Norick Arena. It looms over the grounds, its rounded contours smooth and polished. It's a place for professionals.

"Damn, Ruthie. You're here."

"I know it."

"Are you scared?"

"Oh, hell no." She looks at him, reproachful. "I don't do fear, Caleb. You know that."

He smiles, impressed, and she forgives him the transgression.

CHAPTER NINE

I NEED TO THINK THROUGH MY SITUATION, BUT STANDING out here in the open is doing my nerves no favors. I retreat back to the Logans' detached garage and sit on my haunches, knees to chest. It's cold tonight. Colder than before. Or maybe my body is losing its ability to fight the elements.

Okay.

Number one. I'd come to hate that truck, but that was before I found the gas can, before I found this road with at least one house on it. They say you don't appreciate something until it's gone. The truth of this strikes me in a whole new way.

Number two. Wolfman has his truck back. He's fully mobile again, but that's not the worst of it.

Number three, the worst of it. He knows where I am.

My guess is he'll park the truck in the woods somewhere nearby and return to the hunt.

I look at the Logan Family Lodge, hating it, hating them. I'm right here, right next to what should be safety. It's bizarre, but as disgusting and evil and terrible as the Wolfman is, I can't help but feel he's unable to control himself. It seems to me he makes up bizarre excuses to make it okay for him to kill and rape, because he can't stop himself from killing and raping. Whether born or made, the Wolfman is more creature than human. He's a monster. These people pretend to be decent people, with their fancy mountain cabin and their all-American good looks, but their core is just as rotten as the Wolfman's.

Then I realize my back's up against a wall. Figuratively, but also literally. On the other side of that wall is the Logans' car. If I'm lucky, I'll be able to steal my second vehicle of the day. I decide that I won't ever give it back, either.

I check the perimeter of the garage, and it's apparent there's no easy way in. I'll have to break the glass in the side door, reach in, and unlock it. That's going to suck, mostly because they might hear it and do Lord knows what.

But what choice do I have?

Time to grab a nice, sturdy stick from the woods.

The panes in the door are small squares, and hopefully they won't make nearly as much noise as the window in the Wolfman's cabin. That sound shocked the hell out of me. I watch the windows of the Logans' house for a while. There's no movement; it's impossible to tell when might be a better or worse time to do this. Ultimately, the idea of Wolfman somewhere nearby gets me to push the stick through the glass.

The glass is cheap, thin, and doesn't make much noise.

Pausing, I wait to see if anything happens inside the Logan house. After counting to five, I reach through and open the side door. The autumn moon helps me out. The light is dim, but it's more than enough to see by.

Inside the garage is a brand-new Lexus SUV. Clearly, they need an SUV for their adventurous mountain lifestyle. On the plus side, they are neat and tidy to the point of OCD, and it doesn't take long for me to determine there are no keys inside the garage. In the soft light I see the car, a leaf blower, a trash can, and interestingly, some inflatable tubes. There must be a nice-size river somewhere nearby.

I am getting closer to civilization.

The Lexus is locked, and a blinking red light tells me the alarm is on. I shake my head. Out in the middle of nowhere, they have their house locked, their car locked, the car alarm on, and the garage dead bolted. What do they think? Somebody's going to come steal everything they own or something? Granted, there's a sexual predator down the road, but they didn't know that when they parked the car this morning.

Increasing my aggravation is the continued smell of food. I can't get away from the smell of meat and corn on the cob. At this point it's cruel and unusual punishment, the scent of the Logan dinner.

Then I register what I'm looking at.

A trash can.

If I know the Logans, and at this point, I feel like I know the worthless sons-a-bitches pretty well, they'll have thrown away a lot of perfectly good food.

I pop open the trash can lid, and the smell of food intensifies. The reek of garbage is there too, but all I care about is the food. Tearing open the tidy white plastic trash bag on top, I hit the mother lode. There's balled-up napkins and other gross things, but I don't even have to dig to pluck out an uneaten half rack of ribs.

They've thrown away ribs!

Sitting cross-legged on the concrete floor, I tear into the meat. It's beef and it's fresh. They must have thrown it away right before I got here. The power of food overwhelms me. It's been so long since I've eaten, it feels like a whole new experience. It absorbs me completely, takes over me. All I want is this food, to eat every single morsel on every single bone. Fear, rage, pain—all of it is hidden by hunger and the act of satisfying that hunger.

Even as I eat, I can't believe I'm eating something so good. My family has money, but maybe because we're country people, we know better than to throw away food. Especially quality beef ribs like these.

The bad thing about ribs, they require a lot of work for not so much meat. When I finish the half rack, I dig back into the trash bag and find something even better. A whole baked potato, still wrapped in tinfoil. Returning to my seat on the floor, gnawing on the potato, I think of nothing but getting as much food down my throat as I can. This potato doesn't taste as good as the ribs; it's plain and dry. But it's a big chunk of food, and it's a ton of carbs.

Protein and carbs, some sugar from the barbeque sauce. Simple things transformed into a magical potion that can give me energy, give me strength, let me live to see another day.

Back into the trash bag, there are no more easy pickings, but there are still things to eat. I'm chewing on a half-eaten corn on the cob when I hear footsteps.

My first fear is the Wolfman.

But these footsteps are stupidly loud on the concrete driveway.

I think, *This is Logan.* Like an animal, a growl rises in my throat. I'm not finished feeding. This ridiculous, hateful man needs to wait for me to finish feeding.

My suspicion is confirmed by the heavy, mechanic jolt of the garage door coming to life, complete with overhead light turning on. I doubt the Wolfman has the Logans' garage door opener.

The side door waits for me. I look at it, and it seems to look back and say, "You need to run now. Run through me, out into the woods." But something inside me snaps, and I say to the side door, "No, I'm finishing my corn first."

And that's how Mr. Logan finds me, leaning against his trash can, eating his corn on the cob. At my feet are the bones of my victims, plus some tinfoil.

His arm is extended; in his shaking hand he holds his big-boy gun. It's way too much weapon for him. My guess is, he's never fired it. Has no idea the kind of kickback he's going to get. If he did, he'd have both hands on it. A bigger idiot I've never met.

"You're a menace," I say, as if I owned the place and he was the intruder. Somewhere deep, deep down a little thought bubbles up. *You've gone crazy,* it whispers. I respond, *Yes, yes I have.*

"You need to leave," Mr. Logan squeaks.

Instead, I pluck out an uneaten rib from the trash and begin to strip it of its flesh.

"You need to leave!"

"Why?"

"You're either on meth, or you're telling the truth and you'll bring that man here!"

"I've already brought that man here. Didn't you see that truck drive away? That was him." I drop the bone onto his nice, clean, concrete floor and grab another rib. "He knows where I am now. I'm guessing he's parked the truck and is on foot." I gesture with my rib. "He's probably right behind you."

Mr. Logan swings around, pointing the gun toward the road.

"That's smart," I say. "That's where you need to be pointing that thing. Toward him."

There's some movement off to the left. It's nothing but the shadow of a limb swayed by the breeze, but Mr. Logan fires. One-handed. The recoil almost knocks him off his feet. He drops the gun and clutches his ears. My ears are ringing too, but I just keep eating.

"Surprising, isn't it? The first time you fire one."

Trying to recover, he picks up his gun and points it at me.

"You!" There's a new level of fear in him now. His eyes bulge from their sockets. "It's *you* he wants. He'll leave us alone if you're not here. You need to leave!"

Right before it happens, I sense Mr. Logan has hit his breaking point, and I bolt for the side door.

I'm one stride into my escape when he starts shooting up the place. He can't aim, and so the first thing he shoots is his own car. The alarm blares into the night. The second thing he shoots is the concrete floor. By the time he gets to the third shot, which I think goes sailing off into the woods somewhere, I'm out the side door and into the forest.

I don't really hurry. For one thing, I can't. My feet are in a new kind of pain, one I haven't figured out how to deal with yet.

For another, I know Mr. Logan's beating a fast retreat back to his house. He accomplished what he came to do, and now that his car alarm is screaming the news of my presence to the Wolfman, I have to get away.

On the other hand, maybe the car alarm will lure Wolfman to the Logan Family Lodge, and he can work out some of his aggression on them.

A girl can hope.

Oh my, the little whisper bubbles again, *you* have *gone crazy.*

"Damn straight," I mutter aloud to no one, and then laugh.

Thirty-One Years Ago

THE CASHIER DOESN'T WANT TO TOUCH HIS HANDS. SHE halfway throws the change at him, leaving the man to scoop up the coins from the counter. His fingers leave dirty streaks on the white Formica.

It's not the dirt the woman is afraid of, but the red-yellow stains on the palms, along the nail beds. He wants to tell her it's just iodine; it's nothing to be scared of. The summer rains have hit harder than usual, and the whole herd has hoof rot. He's the new guy, so he's the one who gets to wrestle the dairy cows one by one, applying the burning unguent to their sore feet. It's a hell of a job, one he won't even get to keep. The dairy farm is up for sale. Developers are already circling, ready to create a subdivision filled with cookie-cutter homes the likes of which the man will never be able to afford, and would really like to set on fire.

He likes that thought. Setting those homes on fire. The crackle, the smoke, the pretty embers. But those homes don't even exist yet, so he can hardly set them on fire. He settles for giving the lady behind the counter a nasty look and hunkers down with his corn dogs.

The Stop and Go has five little booths inside it, and the man eats lunch here almost every day. It's the kind of gas station/convenience store/diner combo he grew up with, feels comfortable inside. The Stop and Go even has the benefit of being surrounded on three sides by a rundown farm. The muddy pastures hold a strange assortment of livestock collected by an old kook of a man. Emu, alpacas, pigs from Vietnam. Farms, even weird ones, make sense to the man.

The big downside is that the Stop and Go is the only gas station for miles. He's had to learn to ignore the electronic dings as the people come in to pay for their gas, buy their candy bars and their sodas. He keeps his head down and his focus on his corn dogs and his Coca-Cola.

But then a voice reaches through his protective bubble.

"I want it. I want it, Daddy." Her father mumbles something the man doesn't hear, but he hears her reply. "I said I want it."

That voice slices through his defenses, into his ears, down deep into his brain.

More male mumbling and then: "But I love the Dukes of Hazzard*!"*

Somehow, he knows. He knows before he raises his head what she looks like. He knows how rotten she is. How spoiled and evil and terrible. He knows what she's going to spend the rest of her life doing, how she is going to treat her children. He knows all of this, and he knows he is not wrong.

He looks up, and she is precisely as he expected. Tiny little body wearing daisy dukes cut so her ass cheeks show. Fourteen if she's lucky, but the kind who already has an eighteen-year-old boyfriend. Her red hair is parted down the middle and put into two cute little pigtails. God, how he wants to rip those pigtails straight out of her head.

She's putting on a Dukes of Hazzard *baseball cap. Her father looks downtrodden, weak, destroyed. A neutered man. Once upon a time someone told the man to blame the fathers in such situations, but he never bought into that idea. It's not the father's fault. It's her fault and no doubt the mother's fault too. The mother isn't around, but the man knows she is just like her daughter.*

The girl shifts the ball cap to a jaunty angle. She looks into the small mirror next to the sunglasses and lets her mouth hang open a little, trying to look sexy. She is disturbingly successful. Pleased by the results, she whips the hat off her head and hands it to her dad. "Buy it," she says.

Slump-shouldered, the father takes the ball cap to the counter.

"Ooh! Look!" squeals the girl, pointing out the back door of the Stop and Go to the countryside beyond. "There's a llama!" The girl skips away from her father. "I'm going to go pet the llama!"

"I'll be in the car," he says.

The man gets up from his corn dogs and his drink. He doesn't finish them or even bother to throw them away. He doesn't even wait until the father leaves the building.

The man wants to create that feeling of his brain being popped into place, and he believes he knows how he can make it happen. He's thought a lot about it and then, without warning, she came into his life to tell him it was time to try. Time to find out if he's right. He's not the least bit worried about any of the particulars. Just as he knew what the girl looked like before he laid eyes on her, he knows all of this will go smoothly. All he has to do is let his brain pop into place.

◆ ◆ ◆

For three whole days it was beautiful. Everything stayed aligned; everything was free and perfect and the way it should be. Now it's something else. His brain is sliding back into its original position, the cockeyed place where it sits wrong, like bone-on-bone arthritis.

He's washing blood and dirt off his hands in a cold mountain creek. A dirty shovel lies beside him. It was more difficult than he had anticipated, digging underneath the cabin. So little room to maneuver. If he ever had to do it again, he would make a good-size hole in the floor. That way he could stand up and dig. It is a nice idea, but it fills him with unease as he envisions it.

At no point in the process was he afraid. That was good; he felt proud of that. But now that it is all over, uncomfortable feelings start to bubble up. There aren't many good people in the world. The girl wasn't good; he knew that much. But what if her grandfather is good? What if he suffers because of this? The man doesn't like thinking about it, and yet the little thoughts of "what if" keep rising to the surface.

By the time he gets into his red truck to go home, his stomach seems to be sitting somewhere around his feet. This is a high price to pay for three good days. A very high price to pay.

CHAPTER TEN

CONSIDERING THAT THERE IS A SEXUAL PREDATOR-SLASH-serial killer hunting me through these woods, I'm feeling pretty good. The food has gone to work in my body, and it's doing some amazing things. My muscles don't hum with fatigue, also nice. I found another mountain stream, this one good-size, and I drank my fill of water.

At some point I'll get to deal with all the waterborne parasites I'm taking in. But that's only if I'm very, very lucky.

The other thing that's left me feeling better is the fact I've lost my mind.

Nothing normal is in there, that's for sure. I can't think about my family or friends or even the other girls from my dream. Those thoughts are no longer allowed. It's not something to question, just to obey.

Thinking about people is not allowed.

Right-o. You're the boss.

A weird dialogue has started to pop back and forth inside my head, like there's two people in there. It keeps me entertained.

Although I've lost my mind, I'm not crazy. I'm following the road, while staying a good thirty yards into the forest. My thinking is, the road will take me to civilization, and the forest will keep me covered. Seems like a good enough plan, and if it's not, it's not. I've lost my ability to worry, at least for now.

The truck has not yet made an appearance, which is a good thing. I tell myself there's a chance Wolfman has fled the scene altogether, but it's not a lie I'm really interested in buying.

I'm glad I've given up worrying, because if I was in the business of worrying, I'd be worrying about how cold it's getting. It's getting really, really cold. And I'm still naked. This is probably the longest continuous stretch of nakedness in my entire life. Even when I was a baby, at least I spent time in blankets.

Along with the cold, I notice my skin. The drying mud keeps flaking off, leaving more and more snow-white flesh to glow in the darkness. It's probably time for me to re-mud myself, but the idea of crawling into chilly mud does not appeal. It may even bring on hypothermia and kill me. Super-good thing I'm not worrying anymore.

Eventually a wallow of thick, mostly dry mud presents itself. I decide I need camouflage more than I need to stay warm. Clambering in like a sow, I reapply my full-body mud mask. It's not quite as cold as I feared, but it's not warm, either. There's no sign of the

Wolfman, so I take time to pat the mud into my skin wherever I can reach.

Unfortunately, my arms don't work too well these days. Neither one of them is willing to go above shoulder height. With my left arm, the one with the bullet wound, I think it's because too much of the muscle got cut, and so now it doesn't want to lift my arm up. With my right arm, it seems like there's something torn up inside the shoulder joint, along with other damage down the length of it.

So glad I'm done worrying about these things.

The one thing I do care about are my feet.

They hurt. They hurt in a way I didn't know feet could hurt. I've avoided looking at the bottoms of them, because that's a sight I just don't need to see. Better to not even think about it.

Don't worry, be happy, I sing inside my head. *Pick your way through dense forest while listening for any sign of the man trying to hunt you down and kill you.* It's a catchy tune.

How many miles have I walked? I have no idea. My pace is a slow one, at best. If it takes fifteen minutes to walk a mile, how many minutes does it take if you choose your route carefully, over hill and dale and rocks and stumps and thorn bushes and underbrush? Thirty? Forty? Fifty? It seems like I've gone a hundred miles, but this seems a tad high for an actual guess.

Time is tricky out here too. It feels like forever since I left the Logan garage, but that's just a feeling. I have a sneaky suspicion it's not all that long.

At least the mountain sky is beautiful, filled with stars, and I do appreciate that bright, autumn moon.

"Hello, Moon." I mouth the words, wanting to talk to someone, but not wanting to make a sound. It's nice to talk to the moon. Our relationship isn't complicated. I've never done wrong by the moon, and the moon's never done wrong by me. I can think about the moon without crying, or feeling weak, or hopeless. "Thank you for being there for me."

The moon doesn't reply.

"It's nice of you," I mouth. "You've been a good friend."

A moment passes between us.

"A good friend when I needed one most."

The moon and me will never be the same if we make it out of this.

Some time has gone by without me double-checking to make sure I'm paralleling the road. Sometimes the trees are open enough I can catch a glimpse of it, looking like a giant, pale snake in the dark. When the foliage stays too thick for too long, I walk out to make sure it's there. Each time I check, a little bit of worry comes to life. The closer I am to the road, the more exposed to the Wolfman I feel.

There's a punch of anxiety when the road isn't where I expected it to be. It's a good thing I decided to check, as I'd started to veer away from it and into the mountains. It takes longer than I'd like to find it, and when I do, it's almost as if I want to put my feet on it, just for the comfort of knowing it's there, and not leaving me behind.

Once on the road, I look up and see another house. My case of crazy brain clears a little, giving way to a new sharpness.

The house is dark, but then, it's the middle of the night. There might be people at home. If I'm lucky, there are people home. The Logans be damned, I refuse to be afraid of asking for help. I choose to believe that the Logans are one in a million, that most people would help me. Even so, the fancy lines of this new house make me nervous. It's an expensive mountain lodge, like the Logans' place. I distrust it on a gut level.

The problem, more than my newfound irrational fear of high-end mountain homes, is that this house is way over to the left, while the road is clearly arcing to the right.

Do I stick with the road?

Or do I head for the house?

I believe the road is headed toward civilization, that it's the main road out of here, but that's just a guess. It could turn back toward the mountains and go on and on forever without getting anywhere useful at all.

The house, meanwhile, is a guarantee. It's definitely there. There's no denying that.

Perhaps in part to prove to myself I'm not scared of people, I head for the house. And force myself to hope that someone is home.

The house is on the second ridge away from me. Keeping on the ridgelines would take out the intense climbing, but once I'm into the trees, it'll be that much harder to find my way. If I go straight, I think I can get there without getting lost. There's a giant oak on the first ridge, and I aim for that.

"C'mon, Moon," I whisper, and head downhill.

The descent down to the valley floor is longer and far more difficult than it looked from the road. At least there's a nice stream down here. I pause for a drink. I'm tired from the climb down, and I'm dreading the climb up.

As I scoop the water into my mouth, something moves in the woods far above me.

It's not the wind. It's big. Living. And it hasn't stopped moving.

It's to my left, and I hear it for about three seconds before the forest falls back into silence.

My heart thuds at a million miles an hour, but I haven't moved. I've frozen in place, like a deer on a busy road. But I'm not sure moving is a good idea. If it's him, moving will only serve to tell him where I am. My mud camouflage almost completely covers me. I must be hard to spot down here in this streambed. Even so, a part of me is certain that a bullet is about to end everything. The silence goes on and on.

As my heartbeat slows, reason drifts back into my thinking. I am in a huge wilderness area. There will be deer here. Bears. Coyotes.

No, that was no coyote. It was big.

Well, bear, then. Or deer. Thing is, not every sound in the forest will be the Wolfman. Whatever it was, it was a good distance away from me. If it was him, the sounds would continue and head in my direction. After a long wait, I begin to climb uphill. It's extremely steep, and I take breaks every couple of minutes in order to rest and to listen. I hear nothing else on my long, long way up.

Reaching the top of the ridge is all kinds of wonderful. My

thigh muscles burn from the climb, and it's nice to simply stand and rest for a second. Far better than that, however, is the sight of how close the house is. Another hike down and back up again would have been almost impossible, but now I can work my way to the house along the ridgeline without any fear of getting lost.

Yay for no more climbing, and I'm closer. Closer than I thought.

"Look at that, Moon," I say. "Good news."

Then something catches my eye. It's a long ways off, and at first I don't know what it is. It's red, blue, red, blue.

Sound, always on the heels of light, reaches me next. It's faint, barely audible, but I recognize it as rubber rolling on rocks.

It's a cop car, on the gravel road I left behind. Left so far, far behind.

So, the Logans called 911 after all. Something crumbles and dies inside me as I watch the cop car travel the lane. I could have been there, could have intercepted them. My rescue could be happening this very second. Energy drains away from me, as though my feet had holes in them like a sieve, and my energy is pouring out onto the ground. Of course, my feet *do* have holes in them.

My gut told me the Logans would call 911. Why didn't I think that the road would be a good place to meet a cop? Especially when I also believed that the road was the way back to civilization? Why am I not connecting these dots?

I'm exhausted.

I'm so exhausted I'm impaired.

I don't know what to do. I wonder if I should turn around and head back to the Logan house.

Beneath my feet is a nearly vertical hillside. Climbing up it was hard. Negotiating the path down without taking a nasty fall would be even harder. With a huge climb to follow. It's too much; it's overwhelmingly too much.

The house is close.

That means a phone is close.

I choose the house. Because it is easier. No, not easier. Possible.

It doesn't take long, maybe ten minutes, to pick my way to the high-end mountain home. As with the Logan place, the sight of the house makes me feel my injuries, and there's a new feeling in my wounds. A sort of unnatural warmth, a heat that makes me think of infection. I consider the idea that infection and fever are why I'm not connecting dots like I should.

On the plus side, I don't feel my injuries as sharply as I did walking up to the Logan place. Maybe because I've lost confidence that a house means salvation.

Once I'm right up next to the place, I realize how massive it is. This thing could eat the Logan Family Lodge for breakfast.

The mountain mansion has a feeling of emptiness about it, despite the nice landscaping out front. A home alarm system sign is in the yard. I don't like the idea of forcing it to go off, but I tell myself that if the people are home, they'll wake up in a hurry. If they're not, the alarm will bring the cops, so either way, the alarm is a good thing.

The driveway is dirt, which is nice on my feet, and I follow it up to the paving stones that lead to the front door.

Man, this house looks empty.

I try to coach myself into positive thinking. If it's empty, I'll just break into it, and if the alarm doesn't sound, I'll use their phone. My third broken window in the last . . . however many hours it's been. God only knows, at this point.

Still, though, the darkness, the hulking size of the lodge, the everything—it makes me uneasy. Trepidation slows my steps. Is it good instincts, or have I already contracted PTSD from the Logan experience? The front door is right there, but I don't want to knock.

Then, behind me, I hear something. It's small, but enough to send me spinning around.

It's him.

In the trees.

Watching.

In an instant it's clear. He was following me. He saw me head for the house. The sound above me in the woods was him paralleling me, taking a shortcut. He's playing another game, one far more sophisticated than my own.

I feel myself losing this contest, feel the Wolfman winning.

Five Years Ago

THE GIRL IS TRYING NOT TO FEEL CONTEMPT FOR HER mother. They're sitting at an Applebee's, eating dinner, but only the mother is speaking. Everyone else—the girl, her father, the boy, and his mother—just listens. Tomorrow the girl competes. Now is a time for focus, for confidence. But the girl's grandmother has decided to make a surprise visit to watch the show, prompting a meltdown in her daughter, who cannot stop talking.

The girl doesn't say anything. She wants to eat her hamburger and tune out the worried blather, but she can't. The needless whining burrows itself into her mind, irritating it, forcing it to react, to judge. There is no place for this sort of weakness. The world will not tolerate it. Certainly, there is no room for the girl to be weak. It's not a luxury she can afford, not when so much rides on her shoulders. Her father can be harsh, but he's not wrong about his wife—if she had the killer instinct, everyone would know her name, know how good she is. She would be a success.

The girl has the killer instinct. She can feel it, a hard core of iron inside her. It does not bend or break; it does not shy away from difficulty. It is brave and courageous and it suffers no fools. Winners are ruthless. They create their own luck by controlling their environment, making it work for them. It occurs to the girl this way of being should extend outside the exercise ring.

"Let's not talk," the girl commands, bold and declarative.

Everyone at the table freezes. The boy's eyes go wide, shocked at her brazenness.

The girl takes a big bite of her hamburger. Her parents, the boy, and his mother all follow suit, turning to their meals in silence.

CHAPTER ELEVEN

I RUN FOR THE FRONT DOOR AND DON'T BOTHER TO knock. Grabbing the handle, I'm hoping by some miracle they've left the door unlocked. They haven't. The glass is thick. I look around for a brick or a rock or something to smash it with, anything to get inside, to get the alarm to ring.

At my feet is a fake rock with a grinning frog on it that says WELCOME.

It looks exactly like the fake rock my Nana hides her key in. I've always thought it was a stupid place to keep a key. Now I think it's the best thing I've ever seen.

With fumbling fingers, I turn over the fake rock to find the key waiting for me.

I glance back. The Wolfman is in the drive, but his rifle rests at his side. He's not hurrying. Instead, he walks slowly toward me.

The key slides smoothly into the lock, twists easily, and in a less than a breath I'm inside. It's not until the door is locked and dead bolted behind me that I realize the alarm never sounded.

"Hello!" I scream. "Is anybody home?"

Nobody answers. Checking the walls near the entrance, I see no alarm system. That sign out front was a fraud.

I look back through the door. Wolfman's image is warped by the pane of glass, but it's clear to see he's still taking his time. That slow walk scares me. I know what it means. If he wanted to kill me, he would've. He doesn't want to kill me. He wants something else.

"Hello?"

Nothing. I need to find a phone. I look around. The house is huge, with high, vaulted ceilings. To my right, the kitchen seems to form an island, surrounded by vast, open living areas. To the left, there is a hallway, presumably leading to bedrooms, and stairs to the second floor.

I go to the right first, flipping on a light as I run toward the kitchen. The living room glows in a blaze of light, and I regret what I've done. Turning on lights tells him exactly where I am. I hesitate, almost going back for the light, but what's done is done. Best to keep going forward. I search for the phone, expecting to hear him at the front door, but there is nothing but silence. Silence and no phone.

The master bedroom seems like the next best bet for a landline. I race toward the other side of the house, turning off the light and checking the front door as I go. He has disappeared. It's even worse than knowing where he is.

I scan the rooms. They all seem too small to be the master and none have a phone. It's dark, and the place is so big I get turned around, enter the same room twice.

No, no mistakes. No time for mistakes.

I hate the silence. I feel like I'm missing something. Just like I'm missing the phone. I head back toward the kitchen. There has to be a phone. I refuse to believe these people get good enough cell reception that they can go without a landline. What about emergencies? Don't these rich bastards care about emergencies?

Then I see something. It's like stars. But it's not stars; it's lights. Through the enormous wall of windows in the great room I can see lights. This house overlooks a town, a town that looks like it's a million miles away.

Still no sound from Wolfman. Where is he? What is he doing?

Without much hope, I do another sweep for a phone. I decide not to go upstairs. Upstairs feels like a trap. The ground floor is safer.

Searching, I stumble into the master bath. For the briefest of seconds I see myself in the mirror, white moonlight revealing a horrible sight.

Oh God, oh God, oh God . . .

I turn away. There's no time to absorb it. But that split-second glimpse stays with me. The gash in my head, the wound that started it all. Oh, it's bad; it's really, really bad. I had no idea. I wish I still had no idea.

Needing to get further away from myself, I stagger out of the bath and into the adjoining room. It's a walk-in closet, the size of most people's bedrooms. For a moment I try to breathe through the shock of my appearance.

The blur of adrenaline subsides, and I take in what's right in front of me. There's a gun safe in the master closet. It's wide open. There's a jumble of guns and accessories inside, but all I see are hunting rifles. They're enormous.

I try to pick one up, but it's too heavy for me and my jacked-up arms.

There's a shotgun. Caleb told me shotguns are the best thing for self-defense. I pick it up and almost cry. Even the shotgun is too heavy. The weight of it pulls on my injured arms, and looking down at it, I'm not sure exactly how it works. Where's the safety on a shotgun? I have no idea anymore. Caleb told me they were easy, but I look at this thing now, and it's like some foreign object from space, some alien tool I don't know what to do with.

I let it drop into the mess, and the gleam of a handgun is revealed.

It's tangled up in a giant camouflage jacket on the floor of the safe. I pick it up and find it's a Colt Python revolver. It's what Grandpapa carries. It's a gun I know, a gun that's easy to use. I sling on the enormous jacket, then put the empty revolver in one of the millions of pockets.

There are boxes and boxes of bullets in the safe door. I need to get out of here, but I also need ammo. I try to read the labels, try to figure out which bullets go with my gun. A mistake here could kill me, but it's almost impossible to take in the words.

That's when I hear him.

He's on stairs.

But not the stairs above me.

There are stairs *below* me.

There must be a basement. I didn't know there was a basement. This surprise undermines me like nothing else.

He's on his way up. The sight of him walking slowly toward me flashes before my eyes, and it's like I've forgotten, after dealing with the incompetent Mr. Logan, just how horrible the Wolfman is. Seeing him again made me remember. Made me remember the panties on the end table. Made me remember the hose-down behind the cabin. Now I remember what it is to look into the empty eyes of a monster.

He's trudging up those steps. Even worse, I can hear his hand, his fingernails, sliding along the wall as he goes. He's being loud on purpose, announcing his arrival.

His tactic is working.

I know enough to know I'm hyperventilating, but can't stop it. My body is out of control.

The right ammo must be here, but I can't find it.

A door opens.

He's on the ground floor with me.

Now's the time to shoot him dead. Figure out the bullets already and shoot him dead. Get the bullets, load the gun, lie in wait, then shoot him dead.

But there are no bullets for the Colt Python. Every box of ammo is for the hunting rifles. What's the point of having a gun if you don't have any ammo for it? I want to scream at the idiot who owns this house and has all this money but apparently not enough to buy a simple box of bullets for his revolver. It seems to me I must be missing them, but for the life of me I can't find the right box. For the life of me.

My hands are shaking. *It's okay to run,* I tell myself. *It's okay to escape and regroup.* Okay, then. Run and regroup.

Decision made, I calm down enough to listen.

Nothing but silence for a few seconds, then something wonderful. He's heading upstairs. He thinks I hid upstairs? Upstairs is a trap, and I'm not an idiot. All the same, I'm glad he's misjudged me. Edging out to the ground-floor hallway, I wait until he's at the far end of the house.

Sliding out into the open, I'm convinced he can hear my heartbeat. It's pounding against my ribs so hard.

A door right next to the kitchen is open that wasn't open before. There's nothing to see beyond it but blackness. That's the basement. I'd thought it was a pantry closet. It must open out to a back door, which will put me straight into the woods, headed straight toward that little town below.

Walking as quietly as I've ever walked in my life, I ease over to the basement door. Trying to be fast, trying to be silent. Into the black hole of the basement, I discover the stairs are carpeted.

Glancing behind me, I hear Wolfman open a door upstairs and continue walking. He's taking his time, surveying the rooms up there.

He won't find me there, because I'm on my way out.

I'm ninja quiet on the basement stairs. It's dark down here, but not so dark I can't see the back door is right in front of me.

Home free.

I turn the handle, but the door goes nowhere. He's locked the dead bolt. Smoothly it turns in my hand. I try the door again, but it's frozen. The handle is moving—why isn't the door opening? Each time I turn it, there's a click. I can't have these clicks. These clicks are giving me away. But I can't get out without them. Why won't this damned door open already?

Then two things happen in the same split second. In the relative darkness of the basement I see the Wolfman has wedged a doorstop into the tiny crack at the bottom of the exit. At the same time I hear the door at the top of the stairs creak. Wolfman is here. The clicks have called him, and he has answered their call.

I dart away, thankful for the carpet, and search the basement for another door. I see an expensive pool table, a second kitchen, but I see no other door out in this daylight basement. The windows are at ground level.

Could I get out a window? I want to check, but then there he is. He's right there. I do the only thing I can think to do, hide in the kitchen. But this is no hiding spot. If I was a kid playing hide-and-seek, I'd be the first one found.

He's going to find me.

It isn't a question; it's a fact.

He's in the room with me.

I can see him.

He walks past, his back to me. He doesn't know where I am in this darkness. All he has to do is flip a light switch. He must know this. I dread the light, but instinct tells me this won't happen—Wolfman is having too much fun for the game to end so soon.

Better to feel for me in the dark, find me with his hands.

The evilness of him fills me with a new rage.

He's close now. So close. All he has to do is turn around, and he's going to. He's going to turn around.

I'm not going to be raped. I'm not going to be murdered. I'm going to bring him to justice so this never happens to anyone else. I'm not going to think like a victim. I'm going to think like a winner. Because that's what I am. I'm Ruthless, by God, and I need to act like it.

I reach into my pocket, grab the empty revolver, and in one breathlessly fast motion I ram the muzzle up against the back of his skull and yell, "You move one fraction of an inch and I blow your brains to kingdom come."

Sixteen Months Ago

"SUSAN, YOU'RE A GOOD WOMAN. YOU KNOW THAT?" AND the man means it. He means it with every fiber of his being. He met her at an AA meeting. She is half Native American, which he finds alluring, and she is soft, quiet, naturally obedient. There isn't a mean bone in her body, nor a selfish one. She is what a woman should be.

She smiles at the compliment. Not a lot of people think she is a good woman. An alcoholic, she's been sober for one year, but every day is a fight. She looks up to the man, sees him as a mentor. He's been clean for several years. She isn't quite sure from what, as she's never heard him say. Sometimes she wonders if it's something else altogether, like sex addiction. He always uses the word "vice" to describe it, which makes her question exactly the nature of the thing.

Whatever it is, it doesn't matter now. He is a leader in their cobbled-together community of broken souls. He never misses a meeting, never misses a church service. He credits God with pulling him back into alignment. She follows his lead with perfect attendance. It makes sense to her when he says every day is a struggle, one way or the other. You can either live a hard life controlled by the disease, or you can live a hard life sober. He feels the sober life is the better path, and she does too.

He has thick dark hair and a full beard, which she likes, and she also likes how he is big, the way a man should be. She feels he gives the impression of being strong, powerful, fully capable of doing any physical task you put before him. She likes all of that, which is why she's been thinking about this moment for a long time before it arrived.

They are sitting in his old red truck after a night of bowling with the folks from AA. He gave her a ride there, which featured nothing more than casual conversation, and now he'd given her a ride home. The talk on the way home has been much more satisfying.

"I think you're a good man, Jerry," she says.

He smiles. The idea that someone, especially someone like Susan, would think he was a good man fills him with light. It feels like it could come shining out of his pores.

"Could I take you out to dinner sometime?" he asks.

They were like days out of someone else's life. He moved out of his apartment and into her trailer. They worked on the yard and made a wonderful little garden. After a long time of unemployment, he found a job. It even paid well and it was on a farm. His years working in hellholes were finally over. He was back in the country, working with beef cattle. All the dairy farms had long been turned into houses, but interest in organic, sustainable beef made small livestock herds viable again. It excited him, this new way of farming. Every day he came home and told her everything he had learned.

The longer he lived with her, the less he felt the tug of his addiction. The thing was, he told himself, everyone, or at least almost everyone, struggled with addiction. He'd come to understand it, forgive himself, and work on living sober one day at a time. Every day it got easier to live clean.

This new, unimaginable life is all so good. Which is why his heart falls when she comes in the door one Monday afternoon. Her face is all wrong. She'd gone out to run some errands. Or at least that's what she said she was going to do. He doesn't understand how running errands could make her face go all wrong like that.

"What is it?" He sees her hands shaking.

They sit down at the kitchen table, and she puts her hands in his. He tries to quiet their trembling with the weight of his massive paws, but it doesn't work.

She knows. Somehow she knows, and she is going to leave me.

"What is it?" he asks again.

"I'm pregnant." She starts to cry.

It is an enormous relief. So much so he laughs.

"Why are you laughing?" She's stung, bewildered.

"I thought you were going to leave me."

"Of course not. But, Jerry, this isn't good news. I'm too old to have a first child. I don't have a job. You've only had yours for three weeks. We don't have enough money for this. I'm only a year sober. What if I fall off again? This isn't good news. I don't think we should—"

"No," he says firmly, almost forcefully. "This child is a blessing from God." He believes it, knows it to be true, but at the same time, he's terrified.

What if he's like his own father? Or worse, like his own mother? But he feels that with Susan he can be better. In fact, he can right the wrongs of his own childhood.

"No," he says again. "We can do this."

She is amazed at his confidence and finds it contagious. A tentative smile replaces her tears, but she whispers one last time, "This isn't good news."

The next day at work he sees her *for the first time. She is a summation of it all. She is almost identical to the first girl in appearance. She is almost identical to his mother in personality. She is like meth being force-fed into his veins. It is immediate and overwhelming. He forgets the Steps. He forgets to ask for help from a higher power. Instead he remembers that she is dangerous. He remembers the importance of vigilance.*

He finds reasons to leave the cattle side of the operation, showing up at the horse barn. He must keep tabs on her. It is even worse than he feared. She is evil. He doesn't use that word lightly. There were some he killed who he will admit were only bad. This goes far beyond bad. This goes all the way to hell. It's vital that records be kept so that there is proof of her sins.

Worst of all, she's too smart for her own good. She has seen him and she knows. She knows who he is. He saw it in her copper-colored eyes.

CHAPTER TWELVE

I HAVE BOTH HANDS ON THE COLT PYTHON. IT'S shoved up against the base of the Wolfman's skull, and the first thing that happens is I realize just how tall he is. He is unfathomably tall, or maybe my arms make him feel taller than he really is. Either way, I can't maintain this angle. I've got to lower my arms. For a second, as we both stand frozen, this inability to keep my arms up seems insurmountable. I'm scared I'm going to lower my arms, and then he'll spin around and get me. It's all so tenuous, everything held together by the flimsiest thread.

Then a stroke of genius hits me and I say, "Get down on your knees!"

He pauses, and it reminds me of a young horse who tests you to see who is boss. Thing is, I know how to teach an animal who's boss, so I crack his skull with the butt of the gun. I'd never treat a horse this harshly, but I'm not dealing with a horse. I'm dealing with a monster.

He drops down so fast it's like I swept his legs out from under him. My arms cry with relief.

The Wolfman, now on his knees, doesn't move a muscle. He's afraid. He's afraid of dying. He's afraid of *me*. My fever brain likes this turn of events. It likes it a lot.

"Set your rifle down." He obeys.

"Put your hands behind your head." He obeys again.

Even though my gun is worthless, I keep it pointed at him while I stash the rifle in the kitchen broom closet. It's hard to keep the Colt steady, even held level. It weighs probably three pounds. With these broken arms of mine, it feels like thirty.

Rifle put away, I return the barrel to Wolfman's head, so he can feel it. Because this is a revolver, it's easy to see if it's loaded. I've got to keep him from looking at me. If he turns around and sees it's empty, it's game over.

Pulling back the hammer, so he can hear what death sounds like, I say to him, "Walk on your knees up the stairs."

It's instinct that makes me say this. It seems the main floor is the place to be. But as I watch him walk on his knees all the way to the stairs, then awkwardly navigate his way up them, my crazy fever brain is pleased. Very, very pleased.

We get to the top of the stairs and I say, "This was an exercise in obedience."

There's more light up here, and I want to do a search, see if he has my cell phone.

"Turn out your pockets. All of them." Interestingly, a frightening-looking Swiss Army knife and two zip ties are revealed. "How convenient," I say, before pocketing the knife and tying his hands with the zip ties.

"Ouch," he says, when I pull the cord the tight.

"Ouch?" Crazy fever brain thinks "ouch" is hilarious. I double-check all the pockets. No cell. "Where's my phone?" I ask.

"I destroyed it."

"I don't believe you. Is it in your truck?"

"I crushed it with a rock."

"No lying! Those are the rules, remember? When you lie to me, I call bullshit. Do you know how light the trigger is on a Colt Python? Super, super light. Don't make me call bullshit, because every time I have to call bullshit, I'm going to get mad, so mad I might just accidentally pull the trigger. It's so, so light, you know? Easy to make mistakes, when you're mad." I pause. "You hear me?"

"Yes."

"You understand the game?"

"Yes."

"You understand the consequences?"

"Yes."

"Good. Now, I don't know about you, but I'm feeling hungry. I think this game would be a lot more fun for me with some food. So, you lie facedown"—I nudge him with the barrel and he complies—"and I'm going to go get something."

He's only five feet from the kitchen. Digging around for food, I find a nice, long kitchen towel and bring it back to him.

"You've stared at enough girls in your life. You don't get to stare at me anymore." I tie the towel around his head to blindfold him. Really, I don't want him to see my gun is empty, but what I've said has the benefit of also being true.

"Get back on your knees. Go forward; now take a hard right." I direct him around the dining area next to the kitchen. I throw in a few circles, to disorient him. Once he starts moving more cautiously I decide he's dizzy enough, and I put him in an ornate dining room chair. I unplug a lamp, cut the cord with the Swiss Army knife, and use that to tie his ankles to the chair.

Rummaging around the kitchen, I find very little to eat. This is a vacation home, no doubt about it. I come across some straws in the utensil drawer, and an idea strikes me.

"Would you like some water?" I ask.

"Yes," he says.

I set him up with a big glass of water and a straw, so he can drink with his arms tied behind his back. It's satisfying, seeing him blindfolded and bound; he looks helpless. Neutered.

A small jar of peanut butter and a glass of water look like the best option I have, and I move my meal over to the dining room table. I press the barrel against his head, so he can feel the gun.

"This is pointed at you at all times. You got that?"

"Yes."

I sit down, gun beside me, and start to spoon up some peanut butter. It's good protein. The water doesn't even have parasites in it. Win-win. Deep underneath the crazy, there's a murmur of protest. Why am I sitting at a table with this man? Why am I talking to him? This is insane. This is wrong. All the same, it's not something I can stop.

"So, our game of bullshit." I swallow a big bite of peanut butter. "Where's my phone?"

"I crushed it with a rock and threw it away."

"Why?"

"Too many calls from Caleb. Got on my nerves."

This stops me cold. I remember my moment out in the woods, suddenly certain that Caleb had figured out I was in trouble. "Caleb knows," I say matter-of-factly, but inside there is a jumble of emotion. My connection to Caleb, his connection to me, is more alive and more powerful than I realized.

"I crushed your phone with a rock and threw it into a ravine."

It's not a direct commentary on what I just said, but it's close enough. I believe he's telling the truth, and I move on. Talking about Caleb makes me feel vulnerable.

"Why was I wearing boots? Where did you abduct me from? I have no memory of it."

"You were in your horse's stall, changing the bandage on its hoof."

"His."

"What?"

"*His* hoof. Tucker is not an *it.* He is a *him.* Go on."

"You were bent over, changing the bandage. I tried to chloroform you. You struggled. I wound up hitting you on the head."

So I did fight after all. That's good. "Was there blood left behind?"

"I put the cotton on your head, soaked up the blood. Little bit got on the shavings, but I stirred it up. Put the rest of the stuff away. Used the vet wrap on you. I know what you're asking, and the answer is everything looked normal. No one is searching for you."

If he used the vet wrap on me and the cotton batting on my head, that means Tucker's hoof was left unwrapped, which means Mom knows something's amiss. If I'm right, and I'm pretty sure I am, people are looking for me.

I ask, "Was there anyone else at the barn?"

"No, it was very early. You didn't trust the other people at the barn to wrap the hoof properly, so you decided to do it yourself before going out of town."

"How the hell do you know that?" Not even I knew that. My brain holds no recollection of even thinking those things, although it does sound like me.

"You told Caleb this at the Denny's."

That's right. We grabbed coffee the other day.

"You were there?"

"Yes."

I search my memory, but I can recall no other diners at the Denny's that day. I can't even remember what our waitress looked like.

"Were you sitting next to me?"

"I was at the counter. You're easy to overhear." He can't help himself from adding, "You're loud. Unladylike."

A shiver curls down my spine. I'd sat there in the booth at

Denny's, sharing a cup of coffee with a friend, with absolutely no clue that a few feet away this creature was condemning me to death because I talk too loudly.

Quiet is interrupted by a slurp on his straw. He's finished his giant cup of water.

"You want more water? You must be dehydrated."

"Yes, thank you."

"You're welcome."

I fetch him more water. He falls to like he's been in a desert.

"So, how long have you been following me?"

"On and off for months."

"Months?" I'm blown away by this; disbelief obscures anger or fear or any other normal emotion.

"I'd promised to stay clean, but you needed this too much."

It's a weird thing to be told, but I think he's being honest, and I want to stay true to the rules of the game. I'll only punish him if he lies. Thing is, I want him to lie. I want the opportunity to punish him. I want him to be afraid of me.

There's a pause as I eat peanut butter and he drinks water and I think of something else I want to ask him. Preferably something that will freak him out. Something occurs to me, and I decide to put it forward as a statement, not a question, just in case I'm right.

"You've murdered six girls."

The blindfold shifts, like he raised his eyebrows. "What?"

"You've murdered six girls. Isn't that correct?"

He hesitates, then says, "No."

"Bullshit," I say, sounding as angry as I can. But I'm not angry. I'm satisfied to have gotten under his skin.

"You've murdered six girls. Is that or is that not correct, and do not forget that this Colt Python is inches away from your face."

"How did you know?"

I lean forward and speak softly. "I know a lot of things, Jerry."

Five Years Ago

THE GIRL TOLD HER FAMILY TO WAIT IN THE STANDS. HER three grandparents, her parents, the boy, and his mother, all of them are hidden away inside the giant recesses of the Jim Norick Arena. She wanted to warm up alone, free of distraction, free from watching eyes, and most importantly, free of the burden of managing their expectations. Right now it's time for her to manage her own.

As she lopes her horse around the exercise ring, she is surrounded by professionals. She recognizes their faces from her American Quarter Horse *journals. Those who live in her region are familiar. But most she's never seen before, and some of them are painfully famous.*

The girl shows her horse in a class called Ranch Pleasure, a hybrid between the working cow horse and the show horse classes. She was drawn to it because it rewards athleticism as well as a sense of showmanship. At World's, there's only one division. Meaning, as a twelve-year-old amateur, she must compete against the most accomplished pros in the game, almost all of them middle-aged men. They wear no-frills cowboy attire, and their tack is stripped down. Silver and flash is frowned upon in this competition, but the girl wears a tight-fitting bright pink shirt. She hates pink, but it looks good against her horse's dark coat, and she likes how it flaunts her size, age, and gender. In this setting bright pink works as a giant middle finger, and that's an attitude the girl can get behind.

Eyeballing her competition, she sees a few are struggling, their horses acting up in the cool night air. It's blood in the water. The more she observes, the more confident she becomes that she can manage a top-ten finish. It's a satisfying thought, placing ahead of these people who don't even know who she is, let alone consider her a threat.

A realist, she knows how political horse shows are. But a top-ten finish is conceivable, and it would put the family farm on the map, bringing in the big-money clients her mother needs. She doesn't realize it, but she's hoping again.

The ring steward calls her number, letting her know she's on deck. She gives the woman a tight nod. A flutter of nerves in her belly radiates out through her body. It's been a long time since she felt nervous like this.

She makes her horse walk, keeping his muscles warm and her own body moving. Gazing into the night, she's not seeing anything but the pattern she'll perform in a few short minutes.

Then a familiar silhouette cuts across her line of sight.

The boy walks out of the darkness, up to the ring.

She faces down a swarm of competing feelings. Resentment he didn't obey her command to stay in the stands, gratitude to see a friend just as her nerves hit, and an odd, new pull she's not sure what to do with.

None of this comes to the surface. Instead, she says, "Hey."

He puts a foot up on the bottom rail, looking far too old to be the age he is. "There's something I want to tell you."

Another round of butterflies takes flight. He sounds so serious, she's worried he has bad news. "What?"

"Whatever is meant to be, will be."

There is a gravitas about him that shuts the girl up. She leans forward in the saddle, not wanting to miss a word. There is a smell of prophecy in the air.

"There is only one thing you can control right now and that's you. The rest of it is in God's hands. If he wants you to win this class, Ruthie, then you will win this class. If he doesn't, you won't. The only thing you need to focus on is riding Tucker just like you've been riding him. You stay in your zone, don't even look at the crowd, don't worry about the outcome."

Protests rise up into her mouth. The idea of winning the whole thing is preposterous. The idea of not thinking about the outcome is almost impossible. Before she can speak, he continues.

"I know how much pressure they put on you, Ruthie. But God loves you just the way you are. You don't need to prove anything to him, and you don't need to prove anything to me."

The protests turn into a lump in her throat.

The ring steward has returned. "Ruth Carver? You're next."

The boy reaches through the rails and puts his hand on her leg. "Now go in there and show 'em what you and that big black horse can do."

She laughs. "Kick some ass?"

"Damn straight."

CHAPTER THIRTEEN

MY CRAZY FEVER BRAIN LIKES THE LOOK ON JERRY T. BALLS'S face when I say his first name. His eyes are hidden by the towel, but behind his big beard his mouth turns into a tight line. The knife is already in, and I decide to push on it, dig it deeper. I recite his full name and address. It might be a mistake, but I decide to say, "I wrote all that in giant letters on the Logan garage. Did you see the cop car head up to their place? I bet they've found it by now."

He doesn't say anything. The towel and beard hide a lot, but there's something different about him, about the way he's holding his jaw, his arms. It frightens me, this change. I don't want to be frightened; I want to be satisfied.

"So, what did they call you? It wasn't Jerry. I don't remember hearing Jerry."

"Ted." It's a tight, single syllable. It comes out coiled, ready to strike.

"That explains the T in Jerry T. Balls." He doesn't nod or act as though he heard me. "You want to know how I knew there were six?"

Long pause, then: "Yes."

In truth I probably subconsciously counted six pairs of underwear on that horrific end table of his, but I want to tell him my ghost story, get deeper under his skin. "After you shot me in the field, by the bear-bait bucket, I hid up against some rocks. I prayed to your victims and asked for their help. You were right next to me, but you didn't know it. You kicked a rock down the hillside, and a buck spooked in the forest. You chased the buck. Then the six ghosts of your victims came to me. I saw them. All so young. I bet some weren't even teenagers."

I don't expect him to say anything and he doesn't. I'm disappointed. I want under his skin, I want to burrow under it and scratch around. I want to make him bleed.

"You buried them under the cabin, didn't you?"

Wolfman sits immobile.

He needs to be provoked, so I yell, "Didn't you?"

In the end I don't think it's my volume but his curiosity that makes him say, "How do you know these things?"

It gives me satisfaction to say, "I told you. The ghosts." I mention nothing of the lines I saw cut into the floor. Now that he's talking, I get to the meat of what I want to know. "Why did you kill those girls?"

"They were evil."

"Bullshit!" This time I don't have to fake the anger. The rage is right there, ready for me. I ask again, in a controlled voice, "Why did you kill them?"

"They were impure."

"Bullshit!" I scream. "They were little girls! They were just little girls! Little girls can't be impure."

Maybe it's because my rage has made my voice shake, but his old confidence returns, and when he speaks, it's with that principal-explaining-something-complicated tone. "Have you ever spent time with children?" he asks. "Have you ever seen how children treat other children? Have you ever seen a bully on a school bus?"

He pauses, and I can tell he's really asking. I don't say anything.

"Have you ever seen a bully on a school bus?"

I decide to be honest. "Yes." But yes doesn't really cover it. I've seen terrible things happen on a school bus, terrible, terrible things. Nothing ever happened to me, and I never did anything to anybody else. But I saw. And stayed quiet.

Wolfman continues, in that hateful, overly patient way of his. "It's when they're young that you can see them for what they really are. You can see their impurities."

I bring the conversation back to the truth. "They didn't deserve to die." He says nothing, just vacuums up more water. "I don't deserve to die." Nothing again. "I think you do though."

He swallows his giant gulp of water and says, "Hypocrite."

I lean forward again, almost whisper, "I don't give a shit what you think I am."

Minutes pass. Wolfman finishes his water. I fill his glass again, and once more he drinks like he's dying of thirst. I watch him drink and keep sifting through my thoughts, my crazy fever brain chugging along slowly but surely. Finally a little light comes on and a ding sounds, and I know I've found something important to say.

"Here's the thing, Wolfman. Wolfman's what I call you, by the way, because of your creepy, creepy eyes. So, here's the thing. You're right that there's bad in everybody. School-bus bullies have evil in them. God knows, there's bad in me. But I try to be good." To my surprise, something catches in my throat. I fight through it, determined not to show emotion. "I try to be good. I *want* to be good. Maybe I fail—maybe I fail a lot—but I want to be a good person. You, you're looking for an excuse to be evil."

I want him to say something, but he is like a brick wall.

"You want to be bad. You want to be evil. You want to do evil things. And this whole excuse you've dreamed up, this purification crap, that's the ultimate bullshit. I call ultimate bullshit on you, Wolfman. What you want is to rape and kill and destroy, and you want to find a way to justify it, so you came up with that crap excuse. You hear me?"

He says nothing.

"You hear me?"

He still says nothing.

His silence sparks my rage, and I jump up and press the barrel of the gun against his forehead. *"You hear me?"*

"Yes."

"You're a coward. You hunt people half your size, you hide

behind made-up justifications, you won't admit the truth of what you are, and what you are is a thousand times worse than me. As bad as I might be, you're a thousand times worse. A million times worse. And I'll admit it: I can be ruthless. I get why the barn girls call me that. I get why you think I'm arrogant and mean. I *am* arrogant and mean and ruthless. But you're a million times worse. Because at least I love my family. Even if they did say those things, I don't care. I love them. I love Caleb. I love them with everything I am and I would do anything for them. I'd die for them. The rest of the world, I leave alone. Unless they come at me first. And you, Wolfman, you came at me first. And now you deserve everything you get."

Then I just sit there and wait. He says nothing; I say nothing. It takes a while. He must have been very dehydrated. But then he begins to shift in his chair. I let him shift around in silence for a long, long time, but even so, he breaks sooner than I expected.

"I need to use the bathroom."

"You can use the same bathroom I did."

It's like he doesn't understand what I'm saying, and he repeats, "I need to use the bathroom."

"And I'm telling you, you can use the same bathroom I did." It's starting to sink in, but just in case he's missed any nuance, I say, "You can sit in your own sticky stink just like I did, Jerry T. Balls."

There is a comedic level of disgust when he says, "You are a terrible person."

"Hypocrite."

Eventually, the shifting stops and there is a new smell in the air. Wolfman's shoulders have slumped some, but his mouth remains a thin, tight line. He looks pathetic and small and disgusting. He looks violated and degraded and wounded. There is no dignity to be found, tied up and blindfolded and sitting in your own mess.

And a part of me feels a thrill of gladness at the sight, for here is a man who deserves to suffer.

And in the echo of that gladness, horror blooms within me. In its own strange way, it's a horror as deep as any I've experienced so far. I've succeeded in taking another human hostage, in making him urinate on himself. I made a plan to torture someone, and then I carried it out, and it satisfied me to do so. As much hurt and hell as the Wolfman has caused, I don't want to be his judge and jury, his jailer and tormentor. I don't want to be that person. I want to be good. I don't want to fall into a big, black pit of darkness, because what if I can't get out?

"Wolfman? Can I ask you something?" My voice comes out hushed, oddly respectful. I get silence in return. "Were you born this way?" More silence. "Please tell me." Even more silence. But I want to know, so I put the empty gun up against his head. "Were you born this way?"

"Born what way?"

"Bad. Were you born bad?"

"I don't know."

"When did you first want to do bad things?" He doesn't want to speak, but I really want to know, so I push the barrel into his temple. "When did you first hurt someone? Or want to hurt someone?" His lips are pursed tight. "I won't kill you if you tell me. And don't lie, or I'll know."

"My mother."

"Why did you want to hurt your mother?"

Wolfman tilts his head toward me, as though he can see me. "I'm not talking anymore. Shoot me if you're going to shoot me, but I'm not talking anymore."

I look out through the giant windows of the great room, at the twinkling lights of the faraway town.

"How old were you when you first wanted to hurt your mother?"

Although he said he wasn't going to talk, he answers immediately. "Six or so. It's my first memory."

I take the gun away from his temple, struck by his answer. I have memories of riding horses from age two. Mom would put me in the saddle with her. I remember the spots on the neck of the Appaloosa she had; I remember wanting to go faster, always wanting to go faster. I remember the breeze in my hair and the joy of it, the joy of sitting in the saddle with my mother.

How strange to have your first memory come so late, so strange to have that first memory be so dark. My feeling is his mother abused him. Did the abuse make him strange? Or did his strangeness shape his memory of his mother? I don't know. The only thing that is clear is that he fell into that dark hole right away; maybe he was even born there. Either way, having gotten such an early start, he's had a lifetime to dig himself all the way down to hell.

I don't want to dig down. I want to crawl out.

I want to get to that town over there, drop Wolfman off at the police station, and go to a hospital. I want to be done with him, done with all of this.

The peanut butter helped some, but my injuries have taken their toll. They've almost—but not quite—killed my desire to ride to glorious victory. I don't think anything can kill that innate thing within me, that thing that wants to win. It's what makes me want to bring Wolfman to justice, to stop him forever. I want to be a hero. Then I look at this rapist-killer tied up before me and think, *I am a freaking hero.*

But there are some things I need to do before launching Operation Bring Jerry T. Balls to Justice.

Although Wolfman may have gone to the bathroom in his pants, I need to go too, and I won't be following suit. It scares me, the idea of leaving him unattended. When I get to my feet, they scream out in pain. My feet are damn near unusable at this point.

After cutting two more lengths of electrical cord from a couple of unlucky lamps, I double-tie his arms and legs to the chair. I test the knots, and they seem tight and secure. But it's hard to trust the knots, even though I've been tying ropes around the ranch since I was a toddler. A loose horse is bad; a loose Wolfman is infinitely worse.

I stop three times on the way to the master bathroom to return and recheck my knots before I finally commit to the plan. Once in the bathroom I keep my eyes away from the mirror. There's no toilet paper. Rummaging around, I find some under the counter, as well as a first-aid kit with a big bottle of hydrogen peroxide. It seems like a smart idea to treat my wounds, try to fight the infection.

After I flush the toilet, it starts to run. The noise bothers me; it's covering up any sound Wolfman might be making. I go back and check on his knots, hobbling every step of the way. He hasn't moved, and the knots look good. Back to the bathroom, to clean these wounds.

The damn toilet's still running. Jiggling the handle doesn't help, and I give up trying to make it stop.

Even though my gun is empty, I keep it right by the sink, as though it could magically protect me if I needed it to. Opening up the first-aid kit, I find it's a good one. Gauze, tape, antibacterial ointment. I find Tylenol and take four, then pocket the bottle.

I want to stay in the moonlight. Flipping the switch will mean looking at myself and knowing the truth about what's happened to me. But darkness isn't practical for wound care. Time to be brave.

I turn on the light.

Someone I don't know looks back at me from the mirror. A tremble vibrates through my fingers as I take off the camo jacket. My head is stop number one. It's a significant laceration, one that would've required many, many stitches to close. The first step is to wash with good ol' soap and water. For a brief moment I contemplate the shower. That would be easiest. But loud. Wolfman would hear it, know what I was doing, know I was vulnerable. No, no shower for me. I'll use the sink instead.

I have to curl my head down to get under the faucet, and prop my arms up on the counter to deal with it. It's the only way to get my hands high enough.

It hurts like hell when I scrub, so I decide it's not a part of me. This is a wound on a cow or a horse, something to be dealt with firmly but gently. Just a matter-of-fact part of life on a ranch. This make-believe helps, and so I dive down deep into the disassociation, so deep I actually say "Whoa" out loud to myself when the pain gets intense. Once clean of mud, there's the flush of hydrogen peroxide. It bubbles like a witch's cauldron. There are a lot of wounds to get to, so I try to be sparing with it.

Before I tackle my bullet slice I head back to the dining room. My feet hurt so bad, it takes a force of will to make the trip. I peek around the corner. Wolfman is sitting perfectly still.

Back to the bathroom again. The shoulder is not quite as terrifying as the head. The edges are neat and tidy; that helps when looking at it. It looks maybe like a horse that sliced itself on a broken metal gate. I keep that mental image in mind. I've done so much horse first aid in my life, this is no big deal. This is just a slice, a simple accident. Not even one with long-term repercussions. This horse'll be just fine, once it heals up.

The toughest part is getting my right hand over there to work on it. I use the counter again as a platform to put my elbow on, so my hand can get to my left shoulder. The hardest thing is pouring the hydrogen peroxide onto it without wasting too much.

When I'm done with my shoulder, I'm feeling pretty exhausted. My fingers still tremble. The game of make-believe hides the pain on the surface, but this whole thing must be getting to me, because why else would my hands be shaking like this?

My feet are next. I should check on Wolfman, but I'm getting an idea of making myself shoes out of gauze and tape. Yes, I'll clean and bandage my feet first, then check on Wolfman. It's a relief to make this decision, and I sit down, leaning up against the still-running toilet. It's time for some deep breathing before checking out the soles of my feet.

They don't look too bad at first. But this is because they're black with dirt. I get up, soak a washcloth, and sit back down. With precision I soak and scrub and lift up flaps of skin and put them back down again. It's much harder to keep the game of make-believe going, looking at these feet. After a while, my jaw starts to hurt I'm grinding my teeth so hard. Soak, scrub, delicately lift, scrub, soak, and set back down again. This is what I do over and over again on all the holes in my feet. I'm sweating bullets, and my heart is beating way too hard. Even though my feet aren't really as clean as I'd like, I don't want to pass out and so I call it a day.

I empty the hydrogen peroxide onto my feet, pat them dry with a clean towel, and use every drop of the antibacterial cream. The gauze is light and clean, and actually feels good. It keeps all the flaps where they're supposed to be. Then I take the tape and get to work. I can wrap a horse's leg with the best of them, and my game of make-believe springs back to life. I use all the tape in the kit, and by the time I'm finished, I'm pleased with the job I've done.

Standing up is painful, but it's definitely better. I go to the walk-in closet. There are no women's clothes, but I put a giant white T-shirt on under my camo jacket. It fits like a dress. It's nice to be clothed, but it'd be even nicer to have shoes. But that's just not going to happen. Time to get creative.

I find some knee-high athletic socks, and I put on several pairs. They're ridiculously too big for me, so I take the laces off some hiking boots and tie them around my feet and ankles, almost like Roman sandals. With luck, the laces will keep the socks in place.

Getting to my feet is a revelation. They're painful, to be sure, but this is doable. This is going to allow me to function. A surge of hope rings through me. With my wounds taken care of and the Tylenol spreading through my body, I'm almost ready. There's one last thing I want to do before Operation Bring Jerry T. Balls to Justice begins.

Fourteen Months Ago

HE HAS NEVER BEEN MUCH OF A DRINKER, BUT TODAY HE bought a case of Busch and he's going through it. The TV is on, but he doesn't see it. The only thing playing is a cut of video on repeat in his brain. His last day of work. Being pulled aside. Knowing right then it isn't good, feeling the lead weights drop into his belly, getting heavier and heavier the farther away they walk.

Once they were completely out of earshot, the boss man stopped.

"I'm going to have to let you go, Ted."

Those words still don't feel real. The boss man went on to say what superior work he had done, how he appreciated his effort and energy, how he would give him a recommendation.

He had already known at that point—he'd really known as soon as he was pulled aside—but he decided to ask why.

"Well, I'm sorry to say this," the boss man said, "but my daughter just doesn't feel comfortable around you."

Of course, he'd wanted to tell the boss man that only a coward, only a pathetic, henpecked man would let his teenage daughter dictate his business decisions. But there were two things to consider. Firstly, he knew from experience that a pathetic man was never going to change. Secondly, evidence came in many forms.

His mind wasn't made up, but sometimes things have to be done. It was easy, too, the way the mind could slip back into old habits of thought. It was nice. Like slipping into a hot tub. There was no denying he was good at this work. It was unsavory work, to be sure, but he was good at it. For the last two weeks, he'd let himself slip into the warm, frothy waters of fantasy more and more often.

The thing was, there was Susan and the baby.

So he would keep himself to fantasy only. He would stay sober. But there was nothing wrong with thinking about it.

Today he's decided that there is nothing wrong with getting drunk and thinking about it. Getting drunk first helped warm the waters. It's been a long, long time since he's allowed himself such an indulgence. It feels good. It feels almost as good as a full-blown brain pop.

He is so deep into his own head he doesn't hear her until her keys hit the kitchen counter. Jumping up from the La-Z-Boy, he trips getting to his feet and manages to kick a crushed can of beer across the carpet and onto the linoleum, where it skitters to a halt at her feet.

The first thing he notices are the cans. How had he managed to drink so much? He has no recollection of drinking that much, but the cans litter the floor like confetti.

The second thing he notices is her expression. Her face has gone wrong again, but wrong in a different way. There is hardness there. He's never seen hardness in her, but it's there now, as unmistakable as it is enraging. There's something else in her too. Sorrow. Maybe weakness.

"I can smell it," she cries. It's the sound of a wounded animal.

For a second he doesn't know what she's talking about, but then he realizes it's the beer. She can smell the beer. There is accusation in that cry, the accusation that he is making her suffer. But he is already suffering, more than she will ever know. Rage sparks down the length of his nerves like a string of Black Cat firecrackers on the Fourth of July.

He watches as her sadness is overtaken by anger. She shakes her head; her mouth becomes a hard line of disapproval. Then she gives almost a laugh of relief. "Well, at least now I know for sure I made the right choice."

"Choice?" Confusion keeps the rage at bay.

"I need you to move out. I can't have this, Jerry. I can't have this!" She is close to screaming.

He's proud of himself for keeping control as he says, "You can't tell me to move out. I am the head of this family." He is giving her the facts, the way a man should.

"There is no family."

Something inside him snaps, but in a different way than he's ever felt before. This isn't rage. This is something else. "What do you mean?"

"I mean, there is no family. I told you it wasn't good news. It wasn't good news, but you wouldn't listen. With you losing your job, bringing a baby into the world just wasn't something I could do. And you've been weird, Jerry. Ever since you lost your job, something has been wrong." She swallows, calms herself. "And now I need you to move out."

The something inside him deepens, sinks down to his heart, to his spine.

She has betrayed him. He had no idea betrayal could be this powerful, this overwhelming. But it is taking him down, like a poison that breaks down every cell in the body simultaneously. He is disintegrating before his own eyes. The worst of it might be how she has betrayed herself. She is a good woman. He knows she is a good woman, a kind, sweet, loyal, obedient woman. Why would she do something so against her own nature? Why would she destroy their family? Destroy him?

Watching him dissolve before her, the woman softens.

"Jerry, I still love you. I will always love you. But I can't be with a man who would bring this into the house." She points at the beer, as though it might jump up and attack her. "I have to protect my sobriety." In a still softer voice she adds, "You were the one who taught me that."

The heartbreak has put him into stasis. He can't move. He can't talk.

"I hope you protect your own sobriety, if you haven't ruined it already." She walks forward, as if to touch him, but he manages to raise a hand. She stops. "Please, Jerry, I can tell this is hitting you hard. Please don't ruin years of staying clean because of this. Will you promise me you'll stay sober?"

Dumbly he nods.

"Thank you."

He's willing to make that promise, because what he has to do right now has nothing to do with staying clean. She has destroyed him, their child, herself. This is out of his hands. This is something else altogether.

Five days without any real sleep. The look of terror in her eyes right before it happened is worse than the tape of the boss man firing him. It's all he can see. The clock clicks to noon, but he doesn't get up out of bed. He's not being lazy; he stays there because this is the best place to think. The man regrets the promise he made. There is one person to blame for all of this, and she must be dealt with. Only a promise to a dead woman stands in the way.

CHAPTER FOURTEEN

IT'S MY LAST CHECK ON THE WOLFMAN BEFORE WE head for the town. Peeking around the corner, I see he hasn't moved an inch.

Good. I have time to think.

I want to load this gun up with bullets before we leave. That was something too complicated to achieve while Wolfman was walking around free, a rifle in his hands. My plan is to keep the gun stuck into his back and have him lead me to the truck. Then I'll tie him up inside the truck and drive down to the town. A tricky plan to execute, but my feeling is, if I fire the gun right next to him, it'll scare him enough he'll comply. That's the first reason for bullets. The second being the ability to kill him if I need to.

The gun safe is an unholy mess. The owner of this place must just dump all his hunting equipment down without even a second thought. The bullets in the door shelves are slightly more organized than those in the body of the safe, but not by much. As I scan the boxes, my disappointment grows. There's nothing here but giant hunting rifle bullets, so big they look like mini missiles. The Colt Python is a .357, and as far as I can tell, there's no ammunition for it in this safe.

I really want those bullets. I really, really, really want them. I'm not sure I can pull off my plan without them. More out of anger than anything else, I shove some gun cases and other crap around at the bottom of the safe. Out rolls one little bullet, one little round for my gun.

Getting on my knees, I dig for more bullets. In the process I find a puffy trucker-style camo hat and put it on. It sits high enough it won't touch my head, but hopefully it'll protect that laceration. After searching the safe from top to bottom, I wind up with three bullets for my gun. That's it. Just three bullets.

While I load up my three rounds, it occurs to me it'll still be important to keep him turned away. The blindfold will have to go if he's going to lead me to the truck, but it won't do for him to see how few bullets I have. Maybe I should stick with my plan of firing one off. At least I can keep the zip ties on his wrists. That's helpful.

Bullets loaded, back on my feet, I hear a sound from the kitchen. So far the only sound I've heard is the running toilet, and hearing something from the other room turns my insides into molten lava. I tell myself it's not a big deal, just him shifting around, but I go ahead and clasp my gun in both hands, ready to aim and fire if I need to.

Stepping around the corner, I see an empty chair. One beat, two beats, three beats, as I look for the right chair, the one with Wolfman in it, because I must be looking in the wrong direction, and then it hits like a fist. *The chair is empty.*

Footsteps pull my gaze over to the basement stairs. He's already on his way down, but he pivots as I approach. He's not just up and running, his arms are free too. I thought zip ties were unbreakable, but somehow he has broken them. It feels like an injustice, and my rage returns once more.

We lock eyes. Raising my weapon, I yell, "Freeze!" like I'm a cop. He ignores me and keeps going.

He's headed for his rifle in the broom closet.

I can't let him get that rifle. I can't.

Slipping forward on my new sock-shoes, I've got to catch him before he gets that rifle. Halfway down the stairs I've got a view of the broom closet, and I was right. He's going for his gun. He's almost there. I can't let him get it.

I squeeze the trigger, expecting serious kickback, but the gun doesn't fight me at all. My little bullet doesn't hit Wolfman, but it hits the closet. Wood splinters in the moonlight. Maybe it struck his hand, too, as he was reaching out, because he snatches his arm back and changes course. He's now going for the outside door.

Only two bullets left.

I keep running down the stairs. I want to get right up next to him, shove the gun in his face, regain control. But there's no control here, there's nothing but panic in the dark.

At the bottom of the stairs now, turning to face him, I plan to yell "Freeze!" again, because that's what I want. I want him to stop. I want him to be immobile again. Before the word flies out of my mouth, something smooth, hard, and impossibly heavy careens into my face. It thuds, bounceless, to the floor. It's the eight ball from the pool table. He's managed to throw the eight ball straight into my cheekbone.

I'm seeing stars, trying to get a bead on him, but the eight ball has done its work. Before I can pull myself together, he's kicked the doorstop out and run away. No, not run away. He's never going to run away. If I could believe that, I could let him go his way and I'd go my own. But he's not going his way. He's getting to high ground. He's either going to come back through the front door, or he's going to stake out the house until I come out, or he's going to set the damn place on fire. He's never going to stop, and that's why I can't stop. That's why I run after him into the night.

My sock-shoes help me, and I'm not too far behind him. This is good. Maybe he's not quite as fast as I thought he was. Wolfman glances back, sees I'm giving chase. He speeds up, then veers toward a ravine. The ridgelines are no place for the hunted, as I know only too well.

He's trying to disappear into the forest and that's no good. He can vanish in a way that's almost supernatural. The whole time he followed me to the mountain mansion I heard him only once. In the woods he's so much better than me. No good, no good, no good.

As I race after him, I make a plan for my second bullet. That first shot I was trying to keep him from getting his gun. That was my overriding thought, to stop him from getting the rifle. Now I want to stop him, period. I just want this to stop. It's not about death or murder or killing. None of those words are in me. The only word I have is *stop.* I need this to stop. And the way to stop it is to put a bullet in his head.

We're down in the ravine, and his hiking boots are helping him. He's getting a bigger and bigger lead, which scares me because I need to be picky about the shot I take. I want to give myself the best chance at success, but pretty soon there's not going to be any shot to take at all.

I decide that when he hits the bottom of the ravine, that's when I'm going to stop, aim, and fire.

Everything's moving so fast. Leaves and branches fly by. My brain is full of what I've got to do, only a tiny portion of it is taking anything in. Up ahead the valley floor approaches. Time to get ready. Time to stop him.

A likely looking flat rock, a platform to stand on, presents itself, and I take the opportunity. Grasping my gun, I wait. One, two, and I'm not even to three and there he is, appearing out of some shrubs and heading up the opposite side of the ridge. He's too far away, but it's now or never and time to hope I get lucky. Getting a bead, remembering to breathe out in one long, slow breath until my hands are solid and strong, I squeeze the trigger.

I don't get lucky.

My little bullet pings against some rocks, sounding like a BB from an air rifle.

He plunges into the brush, and the only thing I can think is to keep following him. Up the hillside, my sock-shoes start to take on dirt and damp; they're hindering me now. Once on top, I can't see him, and it takes far too long before I hear him. He's off to the right, which makes sense. I'm pretty sure that's toward the Logan house, which must be in the same general direction as Wolfman's truck.

I'm after him in a flash, but there's a deep burn of dread in my throat, a fear in my heart that's ahead of my brain. This isn't working. He's outdistancing me. But not knowing what else to do, I stick with the plan.

After a few minutes I pause to listen. It takes even longer than last time before I hear him. Correcting course, then along the ridgeline I go, trying to stay on top of the hills, not wanting to sink down into the valleys. Down there you can't hear. I need to hear him to trail him. A few minutes more, another pause. Defeat is slipping into me now. But quitting isn't something I'm good at, so I keep on and keep on and keep on, until I'm standing alone in a dead-silent forest with muddy socks on my feet.

Dawn is on its way in.

I miss the moon.

And I don't know what to do.

Five Years Ago

"YOUR VICTORY LAP," THE MAN SAYS. HE'S JUST FASTENED a blue-and-red ribbon with gold fringe around the black horse's neck.

"What?" The girl is dazed, borderline nonresponsive.

"Your victory lap. They've started the music."

"Oh, shit," she says, giving her horse a too-sharp kick in the ribs, as though it was his fault they missed their cue. The horse jumps forward awkwardly, and a little laugh ripples through the audience.

At first she doesn't even feel the people in the stands. She is in numb disbelief, and it takes a good hundred yards before she even looks up. Her vision blurred with tears, she can't find her mother. There's a bit of anxiety and a wash of regret that she didn't ask where they would be. She wants to share this with her family, but she sent them away, and now she doesn't know where they are. She's in this all by her lonesome.

Despite the shock, something filters through. People are standing. She doesn't know why, but she thinks it must be dinner break, that everybody must be leaving.

Then it hits her. The crowd is standing for her. The crowd is giving her a standing ovation. The twelve-year-old in the pink shirt has pulled off something almost impossible, and they love it. Even in the political world of horse shows, everybody loves an underdog.

Her emotion evaporates like rain in the desert.

This is a golden opportunity that can't be wasted. She has the whole world in her hand right now, all those rich horse owners and the famous trainers, and it's time to tighten her fist.

She asks her horse to gallop, and the crowd responds with whoops and hollers. Then she puts the black gelding into the biggest, longest sliding stop he's ever performed. It's better than the one he did during her performance, and the people go insane. Spins, rollbacks, and one more stop. The people want more, more, more.

So this is the perfect place to stop. Stop while they're wanting more.

She nonchalantly collects her trophy and the blue ribbon for her horse's bridle on her way out of the arena. The prizes are nice to look at, but there is something else waiting for her. A check for forty thousand dollars. She has just won forty grand.

That money means so much. Not because of what it can buy, not because of the economic problems it can solve, not because of anything less than the power it gives her. There will be no more fighting, because she won't allow it. Who will contradict her? Who would dare say a word? No one. Because she's the winner, the breadwinner, the champion, the one with the killer instinct. The girl in the pink shirt who won over the crowd, made them her own.

She thought she knew what it was to be a winner. It has a new definition now. It is a great and terrible thing, to know just what one can do. From now on she will live with the knowledge of what she can accomplish and the oppressive weight of expectation.

This is what it is to win.

She feels the cost even before she leaves the arena. But she thinks, Bring it. *She thinks,* I can handle it. *She thinks,* I am tough enough for anything.

CHAPTER FIFTEEN

THERE ARE NO GOOD OPTIONS.

I could try to follow Wolfman, who has disappeared into the forest, silent as a ghost. When I went on my mission to steal his truck, I found the occasional footprint and broken branch, but really that was more a matter of recognizing landmarks. This is a place I've never been before. Tracking would mean searching for evidence he's left behind. That feels like a tall order, and he's so much faster than me out here. He's a woodsman, he's got boots, and his feet don't have holes in them. He knows where he stashed the truck. There's no doubt in my mind he's got his handgun in there, and probably zip ties in the glove box and who knows all what else.

Hunting down the Wolfman, in the hopes of taking him out with my single bullet, would mean walking straight into a trap, one he will have restocked with the tools of his trade. Thing is, I didn't do too well with either of my first two bullets. It doesn't give me much confidence I can do anything too useful with the third.

I could go back to the mansion, using it as shelter until a search party finds me. But I'm scared of that house. I think he'd find me there, and he knows the place as well as or better than I do.

There's the Logans. Maybe after their visit from the cop things would be different. Maybe the cops are still there. But maybe they aren't. Maybe the Logans decided I was a meth addict after all; maybe none of them found my message on the garage door. Mr. Logan should have seen it before he found me eating his garbage, but what if he was too out of his mind to register anything at all? What if the cops came and nobody ever lowered the door?

On a purely rational level there's a case to be made for going back to the Logan Family Lodge, but on an emotional level it's a bitter pill to swallow. One that won't go down right now.

Out of the mire of my thoughts rises one solid fact: I am exhausted. I'm exhausted beyond all reason. I am exhausted to the point I can't think. I have no idea what to do, and everything is starting to feel dangerously hopeless. Hopelessness is not an emotion to be indulged. On the heels of hopelessness comes defeat, and even though everything seems pointless and impossible, I still want to win. Underneath my confusion and utter, bone-crushing fatigue, even though I don't know much of anything at all, I still know I want to win.

I want to win, but first I just want to sleep. It occurs to me that it might not be the smartest idea, but in the end, the call of sleep is too powerful to ignore. A couple hours of rest would let the antibacterial salve do some good work on my wounds; it would give me back some energy; it would let my traumatized brain heal. At least a little bit. Before I search for a sleeping spot, I take two more Tylenol to fight back fever.

At first I'm looking for something on the ground. Ideally, something like the overturned-tree hole I hid in before stealing the truck. Ten minutes of walking later and there are no holes to speak of. Frustration is hard to fight off this tired, and the hopelessness starts creeping up again. It's lapping against my throat, looking to take me under and drown me altogether, when I spy an almost-downed tree.

It catches my eye because some of its roots are torn up, but the tree isn't actually dead, and there's not enough room to hide under it. It fell halfway over, got caught up in some other trees, and then kept on living. I follow the length of it, and there's a nice place, high up off the ground, where the slanted tree hooks into two giant oaks. It might be like a little tree house up there, a place to hide and to sleep.

Walking the ramp of the slanted tree is harder than it looked from the ground. It's a big, broad tree, but as impaired as I am, it feels like a balance beam. Once I'm ten feet off the ground, I get nervous and crawl on all fours. It takes a while, but in the end I make it to the hooked oaks. It's not a big space by any means, but it's one I can wedge myself into. Probably twenty feet up at this point, I'm scared of falling from the tree while I sleep, so I take my arms out of the jacket and tie the sleeves to a limb, making it into a blanket-slash-security harness.

There are enough autumn leaves up here to give me cover, and luckily they're a dull brown that matches my camouflage coat. Even my long white athletic socks hide me, thanks to all the mud they soaked up as I chased Wolfman. My hat is good too. Keeps my red hair and white forehead from showing. I don't feel safe, but I feel almost safe, and that's the best feeling I've had in a long, long time.

As the sun rises over the ridgeline, I fall in and out of sleep, shifting slightly now and again, never comfortable but too tired to really feel discomfort. Every time my eyes open, the sun has traveled another hour higher in the sky, and at a certain point I think about how I need to will myself into consciousness. It's not enough to open my eyes for two seconds and shift around; it's time to get back to the business of survival.

But then the deep, deep mud of sleep sucks me back into the bog. It pulls me all the way down into the soft silt of the bottom, the place where eyes don't open anymore, where there is no awareness of time or place or life outside the quiet murk of unconsciousness.

I don't know how long I'm resting in that bog bottom of sleep; I only know I go from black nothingness to a ballroom at the Westin Poinsett in Greenville. It's homecoming. Which makes no sense, because our homecoming was lame and held in the school gym. Not that I know for sure that it was lame. I didn't go. Caleb asked me to homecoming, but I said no, said I had a horse show to go to, one I couldn't miss. The truth is I could have missed the show, but I didn't want to go to a dance with Caleb. He said we'd go as friends, but he didn't really mean that, and he probably knew I knew he didn't really mean that.

Now that I'm here, I'm so glad that I must have changed my mind. The ballroom is beautiful. I've been here once before, for Caleb's sister's wedding. That wedding was magic for me, magic for Caleb, magic for Caleb's whole family. The groom's side paid for it, and I know Caleb's mom and sisters felt like they were in some sort of glamorous southern Tinseltown. From start to finish, the whole night was lovely and fun and filled with joy. It was the kind of night that made me hope for the future, made me think that maybe one day there'd be a wonderful night for me. It was my first real wedding, my first time in a ballroom, the first time I saw Caleb in something other than jeans.

I look over, and Caleb's wearing the same rented tux he wore at his sister's wedding. He looks amazing, better than anyone else. He looks like he'd more than fit in with the Carver clan; he looks like he'd be the star of the show.

Everybody from our school is dressed to the nines, and all the girls wear striking, spangly, sophisticated gowns. I'm wearing the same simple white cotton dress from my wildflower meadow dream, but for some reason I don't feel self-conscious. I'm just happy.

Caleb takes me by the hand and leads me over to the dance floor. He hasn't shaved in a couple of days, which is the way I like him best. It makes him look older; it makes him look like the tough, competent farmhand that he already is. We begin to dance, and I see he's wearing cowboy boots. Normally, that's the kind of thing that mortifies me about Caleb, but not tonight. Tonight I find it charming.

"Cowboy boots?"

"Hey, at least they're new." He twirls me away from him and then back again. "Count yourself lucky I didn't wear my usual shit kickers."

"Classy."

He smiles in a way that is a little bit teasing and all kinds of confident. It's the kind of smile that says he doesn't really care all that much whether or not I disapprove, and I find myself laughing.

"Besides," he adds, "they give me a couple inches."

Caleb has always had an inferiority complex about his height, which I've never understood. He's five nine, which is average enough. More importantly, I'm tiny, so I like it that he's the size he is. I say to him, "I think you're the perfect height."

"Nah, I'm short."

"But look," I say, leaning my head against his chest, "we fit just right." And we do. My temple rests in a perfect spot, and I can hear his heartbeat. Caleb doesn't say anything, but holds me close.

It is perfect.

Then I feel him tense.

I lean back. "What's wrong?"

"Mr. Plumber. He's staring at us."

Mr. Plumber is the principal. He's an annoying man, a stuffy man, very uptight and rigid, but harmless to the point it's hard to take him seriously. I don't understand why the sight of him would make Caleb anxious.

"Where is he?" I ask.

"He disappeared behind those people over there." Caleb tilts his head toward a crowd.

Now I feel it too. Tension. Danger. Looking around, I find Mr. Plumber emerging from the crowd. On his face is an expression of malevolence I've never seen before.

"He's circling us," I say.

"I think he wants to kill us."

"Why does he want to kill us? We haven't done anything."

And now, despite the music and the crowd and the dancing, I can hear Mr. Plumber's footsteps. They sound like the crunching of dead leaves. The crunch of dead leaves is louder than any of it. Then that's the only thing I can hear, and the ballroom and Caleb and everything else disappears into blackness.

Blackness. Footsteps. That's all I know. Except I also know to be afraid.

Opening my eyes, I see leaves. Dried, dead, brown leaves. I feel bark under my fingers. I smell a forest in autumn, the smell of decay, of leaves turning to soil.

Then, in the distance, movement.

Reality is back now. It's fully with me. The sun has crossed the apex of the sky and has turned the morning into afternoon. My tongue is dry with thirst, my body is statue stiff, and my little bit of the woods is no longer mine alone—it also belongs to the Wolfman.

His head is down. He's searching for footprints, moving in a sweeping motion across the forest floor. There's no rifle, only a handgun in a holster. He must have gone back to the truck, and maybe even the cabin, because not only does he have the gun, he's now wearing a fancy hunting vest with a ton of pockets. Those pockets look full. More zip ties, more elements of torture.

He also has something in his left hand, something like a stick, but from this distance I'm not sure what it is.

The sight of him makes me want to cry. He is like the tide. Always returning, relentless, unbeatable. He's getting closer to my slanted tree. How does he do it? How can he track so well? The leaves beneath his feet look like every bit of ground I've seen. How can he look at those leaves and see a story I've told with my stocking feet? I don't know how he does it, but I know that he does, and that he'll keep doing it until I stop him.

Despite everything, despite my own survival on the line, despite the terrible things this man has done, it is with sick dread I pull the Colt Python from my pocket. Shooting at him while he raced for a weapon, while on the run, that was one thing. This is another. This is fueled by a different sort of adrenaline, an adrenaline mixed with a cold intellectual knowledge that I am about to try to take another human being's life. I don't want to do it. I don't have the energy for it. But it's something that has to be done.

He's right under my tree now.

Although the process of silently withdrawing the pistol and lining up my sights takes only a couple of seconds, an entire memory runs through my mind. I remember when we had to put Tucker's mother down. She had foundered and was in a slow decline. It was hard to find the right time. She was such a good horse, the first world champion my mother trained as a professional out on her own. She was family. We called her Lucy, and she was the horse I learned to ride on. It was the right thing to do, but that didn't stop it from being impossibly hard.

I look at Wolfman and I think of Lucy. Lucy lived a good life, was loved and loving, but there was a moment, a moment I was there for, when one second Lucy was alive and the next second Lucy was dead. That's what's about to happen to Wolfman, and as far as I know he has never loved or been loved. He's going to die without the benefit of having lived.

All of this takes less than a second to run through me. As I'm thinking these things, he turns away to examine the base of my tree, and God help me, it feels easier to shoot him in the back than in the front. I line up my sight to a spot between his shoulder blades, and I pull the trigger.

As I squeeze, he turns his head, and there is the tiniest, slimmest of moments when he sees me. I look into those wolf eyes, and even though they are empty, they're still alive. In that split second he is alive and looking at me. I am alive and looking at him. Then the moment is over, the trigger is pulled back, and the gun is empty.

The bullet punches him in the back and he falls. He falls in slow motion, down to his knees, then tilting toward the earth. He goes to catch himself, but his hands fold up, useless, and crumple underneath his weight. There is the crack of his skull hitting a rock. Then all is quiet.

I stare at his dead body and feel nothing but my living one. I feel my pulse, my breathing. My hearing is magnified a thousand times; my eyesight is too vivid, like I'm seeing in the ultraviolet spectrum. I am nothing but a living body, the dial on all my senses cranked so hard they're in the red.

I don't know how long I stare like that, nothing but a living body devoid of thought, but then emotions fill that empty, physical space. My little bullet hit. I did it. I stopped him. It's over. The pursuit is over. Relief is there first, but it's chased by regret. I don't want to be a killer. I don't want this memory in my mind forever. I don't want it. It's not fair that I have this image of a man, dead by my own hand, facedown on the forest floor. I'll never be rid of this, never, never, never. From now on it's a part of me, a part no one else will understand. This moment has made me an alien. I will be alone with it my entire life, unable to escape what has happened, what I've done. The weight of this image suffocates me.

I try to get air into my lungs, but I can't, and my breathing turns into huge, gulping gasps.

I want to run, as though I can get rid of this thing, this moment, by racing away. But there's no getting rid of it; it's sticky on my soul like glue.

"I don't want it!" I scream to no one. A keening wail breaks out of my throat and echoes out across the silent autumn valley. It sounds like it comes from an animal, this cry coming out of me, and it won't stop.

I stare at his still form and my regret turns to rage. All of this is his fault. He did this to me. He's the one who made me do this. It makes no sense, but murderous rage takes over my regret, and I want to kill him all over again.

I want to kill a dead man, and this desire makes me hate myself.

I feel crazy. I've gone crazy. I'm nothing but a bundle of contradictions made electric by feelings too big for my body, for my heart, for my mind.

I want all of this to go away.

I want that body to disappear.

Then, the slightest bit of movement.

My tears stop like somebody turned off a faucet. My sobs turn into held breath. I'm not sure, but it looks like maybe his rib cage moved.

Now, for the first time, I notice something very important.

There's no blood.

My bullet hit him in the back. It hit him square and it took him down; there should be blood. Wiping away tears from my eyes, I get a clearer look. There's definitely no blood. I can't even see the bullet hole.

Shaky, I untie myself from my limb. Without my seat belt I feel dangerously tippy. It's harrowing, making my way down the tree. He's crumpled right at the trunk, and it requires an extra-big step to avoid walking on him. It's strange, but I feel as scared as I've ever felt. I'm scared I've killed him; I'm scared he's alive; I'm scared of his limp body; I'm scared of everything.

But I make myself kneel down.

I touch his back.

It's hard to tell, but then I'm increasingly certain he is breathing. Shallowly, but still breathing.

Thank God.

I search out the bullet hole with my fingertips. The fancy hunting vest is strangely stiff and thick. I find the hole higher than I thought, higher than I aimed. It hit right beneath his neck.

And it's not a bullet hole.

It's the bullet.

My brain crashes like an overloaded computer. I don't get what I'm looking at. Again my fingers slip along the strange material of the vest, which is dull orange on top, khaki on the bottom.

As though somebody else is talking to me, a word pops into my head: *Kevlar.*

This vest is made out of Kevlar.

This fucking vest is made out of Kevlar.

And Wolfman isn't dead.

Six Months Ago

THE MAN SITS IN HIS LA-Z-BOY, DRINKING BEER AND CONtemplating the nature of promises. He made a promise to a woman, but is he obligated to keep that promise if she broke her word? She betrayed him. She destroyed their family before it had even really begun. So why should a promise to a dead woman hold any power over him? Why should it count for anything?

He has felt the power of the promise eroding like a clear-cut hillside. At first he fought it, trying to buttress the dirt, trying to build cinder-block walls to hold back the earth. Today he wants to just go ahead and claw at the soil, encourage it to fall down. It's coming down, anyway. He knows that. He knows it's coming. Why not just pull it all down?

His keys are on the counter. His truck waits in the drive. His notepad is in his flannel pocket. Maybe this afternoon he'll take a drive. Do a little reconnaissance.

CHAPTER SIXTEEN

I DIDN'T KILL WOLFMAN. HE'S ALIVE. HOW ALIVE, IT'S HARD to tell. The feel of his skin disgusts me, but I reach down and try to feel his pulse. He's a big, thick man, a hairy man, and it's not easy to find his jugular. When I do, it takes a lot of pressure to feel the beat of his heart. It's moving blood around his body, but not with a lot of gusto.

Before I can pull my fingers away, his head slides off the rock he landed on. It's not a smooth slide, but instead strange and catching, and I wonder if there's a skull fracture. Maybe the bullet didn't do anything but knock him down. Maybe the rock is the source of the real injury. Up on the balls of my feet, I tip backward onto my rear without meaning to. Holding my face in my hands, I want to cry, but I'm already all cried out.

"What do I do?" I say it out loud, but there's no one to answer me. Only birds and trees and sky and fallen leaves hear me.

His holstered handgun is right by my knee. I could truly end this right now. There's a logical part of me that says this is the best answer. The logical part of me wants to launch into an argument about why this is smart. But I won't hear it. Knowing I'd killed him, for that handful of minutes, was terrible in a way I didn't know terrible could be.

If I leave him here, facedown in the dirt, he might die. Of brain trauma. Of exposure, possibly, or who knows what.

After a few seconds I decide this is okay with me. I will do my best to make my way to civilization, and I will tell people he is unconscious in the woods. They will look for him and maybe save his life. In the end, considering everything, this is more than generous.

I take another second and think about his potential recovery. That bullet didn't go into him. I don't know how much damage the rock did. Why his pulse is so faint, I don't know, but there might not be very much wrong with Wolfman at all. He is tough. He is a woodsman. He is a tracker and a hunter and a killer. He does these things extremely well and should never be underestimated.

Wrestling off his handgun and holster is far more difficult than I would have guessed. My right arm is pretty angry about this, but my left arm, the one with the bullet slice, seems a bit improved. The pushing and shoving makes his body roll over. There's a bruise blooming on the side of his head where he hit the rock, but no blood.

When I go to belt the holster around my own waist, I have to wrap it around two times to get it to fit. Wolfman is literally twice my size. His .45 is lighter than my now-empty and useless Colt Python, but even that small amount of weight feels like a lot. At least the holster puts the weight on my hips, not my arms.

I struggle to pull off the Kevlar jacket, and it's heavy and stiff. It's like trying to undress a dead man. There are long stretches of wrestling with him where I can't see him breathe at all, and I wonder if he is dead. By the time it's off him, I'm panting hard and feeling light-headed. Sinking to the ground, I go through the vest. It's strangely exhausting, just searching pockets. Zip ties, chloroform, a small knife. For a change of pace there are handcuffs and duct tape. More disturbingly, there are sunglasses and a wig. He came prepared.

But he didn't bring his truck keys.

I wanted those keys. I also wanted to keep this vest, but now I know it weighs too much. Weight that would rest on my injured shoulders. Weight I can't afford to lug around. I take the knife, zip ties, and duct tape, and cut the disguise into bits before tossing it into the woods.

There's nothing left to do.

The thought is dangerously draining. Searching the scene, I hit upon his shoelaces. Rope is useful. It takes a while, but I free the laces and tie his wrists and ankles. I give myself a chance to breathe. This has all been very hard work.

Now there's really nothing left to do.

Kneeling in the dirt, I shift my gaze from his motionless form to the forest. It has never looked so vast, so daunting. How to navigate to civilization? How to make this broken body of mine keep going? Instead of the usual fistful of energy in me there's a void. My fight wants to leave me. It's the one thing I've got going for me, my endless fight, my desire for victory. It can't leave me now, because it would leave me with nothing.

It's strange. Having a living, hunting Wolfman motivated me. Having a limp, lifeless Wolfman leaves me empty, without strength. Maybe it's not rational, but the forest is harder to face than Wolfman. He left no room for anything but instinct and action. The forest is nothing but space. It allows me to think, to feel, to ponder, but it is cold and uncaring. It makes no difference to the forest whether I live or die, whether I suffer. It will not force me forward, but it will hold me back.

Time to take a big breath.

Time to get to my feet.

Left foot first, then right, I pull myself up. My hearing dulls, my head hums, and something swervy happens.

Bark. Against my cheek. Under my fingers. Blinking, I orient myself. I must have passed out, but I'm not all the way down. Instead, I'm clutching my leaning tree.

"C'mon, now," I order myself. "Come on."

I stagger off toward the road.

Nothing feels real anymore. I wish I had the moon to talk to. It's not here yet. Instead it is endless sameness. Trees, fallen leaves, hills, and rocks. The sun is nowhere. Just flat clouds overhead. At least it's warmer than it was. A southern fall can be cold or hot or anywhere in between, and today is definitely on the warm side. I should be thankful for the temperature change, but I'm not. I'm not anything.

I wish I had my fight. Everything is easier with fight. I want it to come back, try to cajole it. But my fight has nothing to say. Instead, something else replies.

Maybe you were meant to die here.

No, don't say that. I'm going to live.

Maybe not. Maybe you're going to die.

No. I'm going to the road and then people will find me and I'll be okay.

Maybe no one is looking for you.

They are looking for me. My family loves me. My friends love me.

That's the nice thing to think, isn't it?

No more. I'm done talking to you, whatever you are. I wish the moon were here, to comfort me. But he isn't. There's nothing here for me. There's nothing to distract me, and I need to fill my head with something. The terrain means nothing to me. I don't feel anything right now. It's like I don't have a body. I barely have eyes. There is nothing for it but to trudge along, trudge along, until I run into the road.

I need something. Something concrete. After so many days of this I feel lost. How many days have I already survived? I don't know.

I reach back for the beginning, but it's like trying to catch smoke. The beginning isn't there for me. This isn't good. This is something I should know. After fumbling around for a while, I find it. The back of the truck. The shavings and manure and blindness.

Once I touch it, everything gets worse. It's too painful. I've opened a horrible door, and now I can't close it. Recalling the truck makes me recall the cabin, which makes me recall the gunshot, which makes me recall driving through the mountains, and then something else happened.

Blankness.

This is the perfect time to shut the door, but it's so strange that I can't remember what happened next. The door stays open. Tentatively I peer through it.

Then I see a house, a log cabin sort of house.

Lockeys.

No, that's not right. Not Lockeys. Something like that.

Logans.

That's right, the Logans. There's some satisfaction that comes with naming them. The satisfaction gives me the boost I need to shut the door on memories. Nothing good comes of memory. Better to think of the road.

Where is the road? Why isn't it here yet?

The featureless sky casts no shadow, but it must be getting late. I've been walking a long time. The road should be here by now.

It's almost dark. I'm lost. I have no idea where the road is. The worst thing, the scariest thing, is that I'm not scared. That's not good. On a deep, primal level I know it's not good. I should be scared. Scared of dying of exposure, scared of Wolfman coming to and hunting me down, scared of my injuries going septic.

That thought makes me pause. I take a Tylenol.

Once the Tylenol is back in my pocket, I look up, ready to resume my walk. But I'm no longer sure of which way I'm going. Everything looks the same. Thing is, if you're lost, does it even matter which way you were going?

See? You were meant to die out here.

I sit down. It feels like there's a bowling ball in my stomach. It's grief and I'm grieving for me. I can't think about my family or friends or God, but I do think about the fact that I can't think about them. They're right outside my line of thought, and it's a line I can't cross. There is only the tiniest thread, a spider's bit of silk, that is keeping me from death. Remembering my life before Wolfman, before the forest, threatens to snap that line in two.

Need to get up. Need to keep moving.

But I'm still sitting. Every thought is too painful to touch, so I don't touch anything. I just sit. It's not peace, but it's not pain, either. It's the only thing I can manage. Perhaps this is me taking a break, and in a little bit some strength will come back to me.

It's getting darker. Colder.

Deep, deep, deep down, a low, urgent voice tells me this isn't okay. This is going very badly. This can't continue.

But I don't get up.

Instead, I close my eyes and live in darkness. For how long, I don't know. Time doesn't exist for me like it once did.

Then, to my left, something shines; the brightness is visible through my eyelids. Turning to look, I see a line of glowing things. They resolve, become recognizable as glowing ghosts. The other girls. They've returned to me. Tears sting my eyes. I haven't been forgotten. Someone still sees me. Someone still cares. That the someones who see and care are hallucinations doesn't matter. They're here and that's all that counts.

I get to my feet as the solemn procession approaches. They are as silent as ever, but they touch me, and it feels so good to be touched. They reach out and touch my hands, touch my shoulders and face. They crowd around me and love me, and tears fall down my cheeks. I have not been forsaken. Not even by myself.

Five Years Ago

THEY'RE ALL WAITING BY THE HORSE'S STALL. YOU'RE NOT supposed to ride your horse into the barn. You're supposed to dismount outside, but the girl rides all the way up to her family. There is elation in their smiles, in their hugs; there are even leaps into the air, hands clasped over mouths.

The girl slides off her horse.

Her parents are holding one another. Her mom is crying, and her dad wears an expression she has never seen before. They pull her into their hug. She mimics them, raising her arms to follow the motion of an embrace. Then her grandparents take her, hold her close, say all kinds of nice things. The boy's mother grabs her next. She manages to pull herself away, manages to just stand next to the boy. He doesn't try to hug her. He doesn't smile.

"What's wrong?"

She shrugs, but he won't be deterred.

"Tell me."

She lets herself look him in the eye; she lets him see her. "I've got to keep this going."

CHAPTER SEVENTEEN

ONE BY ONE THE GHOSTLY REDHEADED GIRLS WALK OFF into the forest, forming a single-file line. I fall in, relieved to be led. It's not on me anymore. I can just follow, a willing and patient soldier, no longer the captain.

The girls take me toward a rocky outcropping. It's a feature I would have avoided on my own; it looks sharp and treacherous. They guide me into the rocks, to a hidden path that's easy on my feet. We go on in this way for some time, going ever upward, until the path peaks in a grove of beech trees. The trail slopes downward now, and a new sound hits my ears.

It's unfamiliar after so much silence, but I believe it's the sound of traffic.

The noise awakens something within me, something that sniffs the air with ears pricked. No sooner has it shown its head than it has to return to ground, however, as the trail turns steep. Every bit of energy I have must go to picking my way down the rocks. The girls never take a wrong step, so I follow them, footfall for footfall. As we descend, the rushing noise grows louder.

Steep turns to nearly vertical, and I'm forced to use my hands. My shoulders don't like it, not one bit, but I tune them out. All the while the sound grows bigger and more mysterious. I still suspect it's traffic, but something's not right.

There's no room to look around and figure out what I'm hearing. I'm in a crevice of black rock. The slightest mistake would mean a broken neck, especially as the stone turns wetter the lower I get.

The last thirty feet is nothing but focus, nothing but wet rock and handholds and footholds and blackness. I arrive upon level ground to find the girls are gone. I'm not even sure when I last saw them or if I really saw them at all.

One thing is clear, though, undeniably giant and real. The sound was not traffic. The sound was water. I'm in a ravine through which courses a mighty river. There is a level spit of land under my feet. Above me hulks an impossible wall of granite. Had I known what I faced, I would never have made the attempt.

That creature that lifted its head and smelled the air at the top of the cliff returns. Traffic would have been better than water, but this is something. When I first entered the forest, I hoped to find a river. Big rivers lead to roads and this is a big river.

The patch of earth I'm on doesn't look too big. I take two steps forward, intent on investigating this new world, and bump into something strange. It moves away from me with a skitter, too light and airy to be a part of nature. Reaching down, I feel rubber. It's an inner tube. A fancy one too. Almost more a boat than a tube. Thick walled, there's a floor to it. . . . It even still holds some air.

Pulling it forward into the starlight, I examine my find. It has two compartments, fore and aft. The front section is somewhat inflated. The back is almost flat. Without pausing to consider, I get to work on my tube. I blow air into it and listen for the hiss. With my fingers, I search for the hole. With Wolfman's duct tape, I patch it.

The stars shift overhead, but I pay them no mind. Everything I have is bent on my little boat. Blow, listen, feel, patch. When the night has reached its darkest point, the tube sits before me, full and waiting. I pace my spit of land, looking for the best place to launch. Only now do I realize how small this place is, surrounded on all sides by sheer cliffs and fast water. Had it not been for the boat, I would've been trapped.

In the end, no place is better than any other. I'm not afraid of drowning, having grown up as a river rat. I'm afraid of getting wet and getting cold. It's much warmer tonight than it has been, but once I'm dunked in river water, it'll feel freezing in a hurry. Just as I start to overthink the problem, I find my courage and jump in.

The motion is as smooth and seamless as anything I've ever done in the show ring. There's a tremendous relief in the action. Not only did I stay dry, but my body and mind felt like my own again. In pushing off from the land, I felt athletic and brave. I felt like a fighter. I felt like me.

I'm not dead yet.

The water moves quickly, but not so quickly that it scares me.

I pull a floating stick out of the river to use as a raft pole, well aware rapids might make such a thing necessary. But so far it looks manageable, and hopefully it will stay that way.

I let go of a breath I didn't know I was holding.

For a few minutes I simply sit in my boat and let go of a lot. And when I've let go of enough, I lean back and find myself literally star struck.

Framed by rock and tree is a night sky unlike any that has ever been or ever will be. It is too big to understand, but I can't stop trying to understand it. I want it all. I want to take it all in. Every enormous star, the haze of the Milky Way, the deep blue-black of space, it is vast beyond my ability to reckon. Behind me the river gurgles a soundtrack, accompanied by the rustle of the trees. It is beautiful.

In this otherworldly moment I am profoundly grateful to be here, to be alone, to experience this thing that no one has ever experienced and that no one else ever will.

Even if I die, I will have known this.

As I gaze up into the stars, my grandma's favorite exclamation comes to me. "Heavens above!" The sound of her voice and all the different ways she says that phrase—irritated, awed, happy, dismayed—run through my mind. It cracks something open inside me, and all the things I've held back, the voices and faces of my loved ones, my prayers for survival, all of it comes rushing back to me. The wind freeze-burns the path my tears have made.

Without warning I start to sing. I didn't even know a song had fought its way to the surface of my mind, but it's there, coming out of my croaking throat.

"O Holy Night! The stars are brightly shining . . ."

It is my favorite hymn. I have no voice for singing, never have, but I sing it anyway.

"It is the night of our dear Savior's birth. . . ."

It's no time for Christmas carols, floating half-dead down an unknown river in the middle of autumn, and yet this carol wants to be sung.

"A thrill of hope the weary world rejoices . . ."

It's not the right line. The song is coming out fractured, broken. I don't care. I just sing whatever line presents itself.

"Fall on your knees! Oh, hear the angel voices! / O night divine, the night when Christ was born . . ."

I fall silent. I think the singing is over, but then the chorus rises up within me, and I fully let go of the music, letting it sail all the way to the heavens above.

"O night, O Holy Night, O night divine!"

And then once more, softer, almost a whisper.

"O night, O Holy Night, O night divine!"

As the last line dies upon my lips, the moon makes its appearance, sliding out casually from behind a rock face. He's not as full as he once was, but he remains blindingly bright.

"Moon!" I say. "Oh, Moon, it's good to see you."

It's good to see you, too, he seems to say to me. *You're alive.*

"I am."

It's good to be alive.

"Yes, it is."

Take courage and rest. I will watch out for you.

"Thank you, Moon."

The night returns to the music of the river and the trees. I half shut my eyes and open my ears, listening for the sound of rapids. I don't worry, though. The moon is protecting me. If rapids are ahead, I'll hear them and it will be okay. It's important to rest, to feel whatever peace is available to me. Who knows how long it will last.

I wake up, curled into a ball at the bottom of my boat. There's no memory of how my night ended, but I've run aground in a shallow tributary. The main river is to my right, only a few feet away. The sun is up, and today promises to be even warmer than yesterday. My socks have dried, which is nice.

I wobble in my boat, but manage to step off onto some rocks and keep my socks dry. I drink deeply from the small creek, which helps. The water is crystal clear and cold. The big river draws me to it, as though it might explain some things to me. My thigh muscles quiver, so do my arms. Walking isn't as easy as it once was. I reach the bank, but the water doesn't have much to say. The forest is so high and thick, it's impossible to get a sense of where I am or how far I've traveled downriver.

Alongside the waterway are giant boulders. I reach out a hand, wanting to steady myself, and see a little miracle down by the water's edge. Mussels. Freshwater mussels. And there are a lot of them. I fish out the knife and get to work on the mollusks.

It is bliss eating the mussels. Not just because they're food and I desperately need to eat, but because the act of finding them, cracking them open, and swallowing them takes every bit of brain power I have. It's something to do and it is all consuming. The distraction is as delicious as the protein sliding its way into my belly.

I eat every single mussel I can find. By the end I'm full, even though a week ago it would have been a light meal at best. A rounded rock looks like a good place to sit down and digest. As I look out over the river, last night returns to me. The sight of the stars and the moon, the ability to remember the faces of my family; something healing happened last night. Something corrective.

The paranoid idea that my family would not be looking for me seems ridiculous now, in the light of day. Of course they're looking for me. Whether or not I'll ever be found, I don't know. But the certainty that they're searching for me rests in my heart.

A physical ache that has nothing to do with my injuries fills me. It's the bone-deep desire to tell them how much I love them, to tell them I'm alive. This is what I have been protecting myself against, the overwhelming agony of knowing how much they must be hurting. I wish I could tell them it's okay. I wish I could tell them what I've learned. I wish I could tell them how sorry I am.

The idea comes to me that if I pray hard enough, their souls will hear mine. If I've learned nothing else out here, I've learned that there are mysteries that cannot be accounted for. Had it not been for the hallucination of the redheaded girls, I would never have made it down that cliff, never would have found my boat. So I believe there's a chance my prayers will be heard.

"Mommy," I begin. I haven't used that name since I was five. "Mommy, I want you to know I love you and I'm alive. I want you to know I'm sorry for all the things I've ever done. For being mean to the other girls at the farm and for being too hard to deal with. I really didn't know what I was doing. I really didn't. But I do now, and if I get a chance to live life again I'll be different. I swear to God I'll be different. I'll be a good daughter. I promise I'll be good."

Tears threaten to shut down my throat, but I force myself to keep going.

"Daddy, I love you with all my heart. I know you're looking for me. Please keep looking. Please go to the mountains. I'm in the mountains, Daddy. I'm alive and I love you and I want to see you more than anything. I will never argue with you again, I promise. I know I used to argue over every little thing, but I really didn't know what I was doing. I thought I was doing right; I really did. I know better now."

"Grandpapa and Nana, I'm so sorry. I guess I didn't fight hard enough. You believed in me, and you always told me I was strong enough to do anything. But I want you to know I've tried my best. I've given it everything I've got. Sometimes that hasn't been very much. I guess I'm not quite as strong as we thought I was. But I'm not giving up. I'm still alive, and I'm not giving up. Not until I'm dead. I love you, Nana and Grandpapa. You've never been anything but good to me, and I love you so much."

The next person in line sobers me up a little. "Grandma, I know you don't totally get me. I don't totally get you, either. But I love you. If I get out of here, things will be better between us. I'll be open-minded and go shopping with you. I love you, Grandma."

Finally my mind turns to a face outside my family, and for a while all I can do is cry. "Caleb. I am so, so, so, sorry. I've been a coward. I've been mean. I've been selfish. I have no idea why you love me. I don't deserve you. I never have. I want you to know that if I get out of here, it will be different. I've always thought I was so tough and strong, but I've never been brave enough to love you back, even though I love you in my heart. I've always been too worried about what other people would think, what my family would think. From now on, I'm going to be brave. I promise you, I am going to be brave. I love you, Caleb. I'm so sorry."

Having said my confession prayers, I feel better, clearer, stronger. It seems a natural idea to keep going downriver, hoping to hit a highway. Pulling my boat out, I find it's gone a bit flat. I add air and patch up areas that seem leaky.

My raft pole is still with me, which is good. It's nice and straight, without any rot. As I get into my boat and set off, the sun at my back, everything seems brighter. I've escaped Wolfman. I've lived a day alone in the wilderness. I've eaten a good bit of protein, and there's plenty of water to keep me hydrated. I'm confident this river will eventually lead me to a road.

It strikes me as strange how despairing I was twenty-four hours ago. Maybe it was hunger, or exhaustion. Maybe it was just the fact I'd lost faith. No matter the cause, I've been cured. For the first time since I found myself in the back of the truck, the odds are in my favor. I will get out of here. I will survive. My fight is back, and once again I can taste victory.

I said my confession prayers and meant every word, but I cannot help but imagine what it will be like to find my rescuers. They will be amazed that I survived, that I beat the odds. They will be blown away by the fact that I defeated a serial killer at his own game. I won't say it out loud, because that would be too much, but on the inside I'll think, *I am Ruthless, and I'm no one to be trifled with.*

Ten Days Ago

HE SITS AT THE COUNTER OF THE DENNY'S, LISTENING TO the target go on and on about herself. There is the entertaining thought of spinning around, leaping upon her, and stabbing her in the neck. Satisfying, in its own way, but the repercussions would be too severe. Besides, what would she learn from that? Nothing. There must be some purification for her, too. It's not all about him and his needs. There should be a balance struck. To be fair, it is also about his own needs, and considering how very, very long it's been, he's planning on taking his time. He's going to make this into a special vacation for himself.

Right now his plan is to return to sobriety after this job is over. Way, way down, deep underneath, he senses that once his sobriety is blown, it will be hard, maybe even impossible, to get back on the wagon. There's a vague discomfort with this, so it's best to keep believing that this is a one-time gig.

For twenty minutes now it has been nothing but the target pretending she's not flirting with the boy. The man finds the kid interesting. He's obviously smart. There's a perceptive look about him, so why does he tolerate her torture? The man shakes his head. He is going to be doing this boy an enormous favor. Sure, he'll be upset at first, but in the long run he'll be thankful.

At last, something of note. The target complains about her horse's injured hoof, how no one is competent enough to wrap the foot correctly. She complains about entrusting her mother with the task during her absence. She complains about how she is going to have to get up so early before she goes to the beach to take care of the injury one last time.

He is profoundly grateful. Truth be told, he continued to have some doubts about whether it was right for him to break his promise. But here the stars have aligned; they have come together to tell him that this is meant to be. Providence never lies.

CHAPTER EIGHTEEN

IT'S SOMETIME IN THE AFTERNOON WHEN I DECIDE TO get off the river. The day is pleasantly warm, probably close to seventy degrees. The river has been nothing but smooth sailing. It's hard not to feel anxious about how long I've traveled without hitting a road, but I'm trying to have faith. A road will come. I know it will.

After I pull my boat out of the water, I use the forest as a bathroom. Not comfortable, but I see it as a good sign. My body is returning to normal. This is good. This is hopeful.

If only I was at the road already. . . .

Nope. Not going to think about that. Instead, I search for mussels. I find a handful, but no more. My morning feast was a lucky break. There are minnows darting in and out of the shallows. I want to catch and eat them, but it's a temptation that should be resisted. Trying to catch little quicksilver fish would be a good way to waste time and calories. Instead, I make repairs to my boat.

It's time to get back on the river. Just as I step into the tube, I hear the baying of hounds. It's far, far off. I can barely hear it, but it's definitely the sound of hunting dogs.

Or maybe the sound of search-and-rescue dogs.

"HELLO!" I scream so loud it hurts my throat.

Nothing.

"HELP!"

Nothing.

"HELP!"

It's pointless. You can hear a good coonhound from five miles away. The human voice doesn't travel like that. Especially not over the sound of a river. I strain to hear, pacing up and down the riverbank, but the hounds are gone.

The work I did on the Logans' garage door has borne fruit. There are people searching for me, but they're searching upriver. Far upriver. Or maybe not. Maybe those were hunting dogs. It is hunting season; it would make sense.

I don't know and I wish did. I have one foot in my boat. Either I get in and keep going in hopes of finding a road, or I start the trek back toward the baying hounds, hoping to find rescuers.

There's no good answer.

Ultimately, I decide on the boat. Hiking upriver would be difficult, maybe even impossible. The boat is relatively easy, and I've found a source of food on the river. I get in and push off, praying that a highway is around the next bend.

◆ ◆ ◆

I've heard the faint baying of hounds one more time, but that was a while ago. After that, a rifle shot, but that came from another direction. Even so, the sound of hunters makes me doubt my search-and-rescue idea. Ever since the gunshot it has been nothing but the sounds of the forest, the sounds of the water. Very slow, very shallow water. I have to use my raft pole to keep my boat moving forward. Going downriver feels like a mistake. An enormous mistake. But would it be an even bigger one to abandon course and go back?

My arms get tired as I use my raft pole again and again, pushing away from boulders and back into the current. Up ahead there's a sharp turn in the river. On the other side of that hairpin corner I want to see a bridge. A nice, clean, fancy bridge. The kind that big highways have. I want that bridge so bad, I think I can will it into existence.

It takes a thousand years to get to that bend. Slow, shallow, bumping, barely moving water holds me back, but every minute is spent envisioning that bridge. Willing it to be there. I can see the spans, the angle of it, the color of the concrete, the shadows cut by the sun.

Reaching the turn in the river, I hear something. It might be traffic.

Once around the corner I see it's not traffic. It's white water.

Before I can map a plan, I'm in the rapids. Ice water slaps me across the face. I sputter to clear my mouth, attempt to wipe the water from my eyes. As soon as I'm clear, I'm slapped again. My boat turns sideways, then backward. I'm going down blind. I remember my stick and shove off from a boulder hard. Both shoulders scream. Twisting back to sideways now. Just as I get a glimpse of where I'm going, I slam against a rock. The back of my head hits granite. My concussion flares.

"No!" I say to no one but the river, but all the same, I say it. This damn river isn't going to be what beats me, not after facing down a serial killer on his own ground.

I push against another rock. My boat spins. I hit another rock, steadying myself. Now that I'm facing forward again, I put my stick across my lap, ready to push off left or right. Looking down the gauntlet of the river, I map a course. There's a channel of smoother white water down the center. Two quick moves with my stick gets me there. A second of peace lets me get to my knees. Now I can use my weight to keep balance.

Riding this river feels like sitting on a bucking two-year-old horse. When a young horse explodes, there's always a second where you don't know what the hell is going on, but then you find the rhythm of it. There's no time to be scared, there's only time to react. That's what I do, down the white water. React. Push, push, shift, push, shift, shift. My weight and my raft pole, that's all I've got. I'm starting to get a handle on how to do this when a strange sound begins to thrum overhead.

It's loud, mechanical, not from nature.

Thrum. Thrum. Thrum.

I can't look away from the river, so I only catch a glimpse. A helicopter. Headed upriver, toward the baying hounds. In less than a second it's gone.

A boulder rises up out of nowhere. No time to think about the helicopter. No time to think I'm wearing a camouflage hat and jacket. No time to think I'm invisible against the pattern of dark green water, white rapids, and boulders. No time to think that this river is taking me a million miles away from help. No time to think that no matter how hard I try to do right, all I make are mistakes.

There's no time to think these things, but I think them anyway. I'm riding the wild, bucking river, but it's my animal brain guiding my body. The real me is floating away, with the helicopter, up into the sky.

The river quiets for a minute. Not so quiet as to be safe, but it's not nearly as treacherous. I catch my breath. Wipe water from my face. Rest.

I think the rapids are over.

They're not.

I come around yet another bend, and there's a damn-near waterfall waiting for me.

"Oh shit." It almost strikes me as funny. I sound resigned, weary, like someone irritated by spilled milk. But this isn't spilled milk. This is quite possibly my death.

The only thing I can do is get centered and steady and hold on to my stick. My stomach drops out from underneath me before the river does. Miraculously my little boat stays facing forward. Down into the froth and back out again, down three more levels of rapids, the whole thing goes as smoothly as it possibly could.

Now the river truly quiets. But I'm not quiet. I'm laughing. I just survived a mother-effing waterfall. How the hell did I do that?

I have no idea; but I'm glad I did. Having ridden a waterfall all the way down takes the sting out of seeing the helicopter. Right now it's much easier to have faith in providence, to believe that I am where I'm supposed to be.

The sun is about to dip behind the mountains. My friend the moon is going to pay me a visit sooner rather than later, and a visit from a friend is always nice. Before all sunlight is lost, I pull up to a nice, sandy bank. It's a good place to work on my boat. It's worse for wear after going through the rapids. It takes quite a while to get it pumped up again. By the end I'm feeling a bit weaker than I'd like to. Unfortunately, there are no mussels around.

Sitting there, I don't think about being hungry, or what else I might find to eat. At least I don't consciously think about it. But then something clicks in my mind, and I realize I'm looking at dandelions. The flowers are long gone, but the leaves remain. I've heard stories of dandelion tea, though I've never had it, and I know people pick the leaves and put them into salad.

These are safe to eat. With a thrill I pick a leaf and taste it. Not bad. A bit spicy, but not anything unpleasant. I want to grab up whole handfuls and eat, but it's important to chew slowly. My stomach is fragile. Besides, the slower I eat, the more full I'll feel.

By the time I'm done with my salad of wild greens, it's dusk. I push off into the water, and my old anxiety, the desire to find a highway, comes alive within me.

Everything's okay, I tell myself. *I'm alive. I've eaten. I have a boat. It'll be okay. I will find a highway.*

◆ ◆ ◆

Something new has taken over my world. Fog. It came on a little at a time, and at first I thought it was pretty. When it was nothing more than scenic wisps of smoke on the water, it *was* pretty. This is something else. This is like wading through wool. There must be heavy clouds above me, because no moonlight, no starlight, can find its way through the thickened air. There will be no visit from the moon tonight. This makes me sadder than it should. I need a friend now more than ever.

There is a new kind of quiet, too. The rustle of leaves and the sweet gurgle of the river have given over to a dead calm. It's as though the only things that exist are me and my boat and the water that surrounds me. I can't see either bank, and there hasn't been any rock for some time.

The river has broadened and deepened, becoming a lazy sort of southern river. Even so, lazy southern rivers can very quickly become raging rapids. I keep my ears sharp for the sound of white water, but the more I strain to hear, the more I hear nothing.

I'm tired. Dead tired. The endless nothing makes me even more tired, while making me all the more anxious. It leaves me not really awake but nowhere near resting, a terrible place of limbo. Limbo is a bad place to be. Limbo is a fertile ground for the imagination.

What if this river just peters out? Just turns into smaller and smaller streams, never takes you to a road?

No. It's a big river. Big rivers lead to roads. It's the way civilization works.

What if the search-and-rescue people give up? How long have they been searching around the Logan place? They won't search forever, and there's no reason for them to come all the way out here.

I know that. The search-and-rescue people won't find me. I already know that. I have to find them. That's how this is going to work.

Still thinking it's going to be this great victory? You come strutting out of the wilderness, a champion? You know even if you do get out of here, you will collapse and cry before the first person you meet.

Maybe, maybe not.

You will collapse and cry because you're broken now. You're damaged goods. You always thought so highly of yourself, didn't you? Pride. You were prideful. Now look at you. Broken. Damaged.

But still alive.

Alive for what? How many years of therapy will it take to fix this? A million? Guess what. You're not going to live for a million years. You're going to be broken all of your life.

I'll still alive and that's all that matters.

But think of what you've seen. The underwear on the table. Wolfman masturbating. Do you remember making him go the bathroom in his pants? Do you remember taking cold aim and shooting a man in the back? Have you forgotten that? There's no coming back from this.

Shut up and leave me be. I've got to be ready with my stick, just in case the river turns or a boulder comes up out of the fog. A boulder is a real danger. I can't see two feet ahead of me. Last thing I need is to break my boat on a rock.

Out of the deep silence comes a sound. It is instantly recognizable and makes my insides melt with adrenaline. It's the sound of a car. A car moving fast, driving on a smooth highway. But it seems to be coming from behind me.

Confusion spins my head around, and I see headlights floating through the fog. The car *is* behind me. Far behind. I must've drifted through the span of a bridge without the vaguest clue I was near a highway.

The car passes over the river and disappears into the forest without a second thought to me or my plight.

Swinging from paralyzed to panicked, I take my stick and try to push toward the left bank. The stick does nothing. The water is too deep for it to touch bottom. I put my arms in the cold, cold water and start paddling. My shoulders hate it, they hate it so much, but it doesn't matter. The only thing that matters is getting to solid ground, getting to the road.

I'm breathing hard by the time I grab on to a tuft of grass. The water is too damn deep here, the bank at too sharp of an angle. A tangle of rhododendron branches reach out to me, but they're only in my way. If my freaking shoulders worked, I could pull myself up and out, but there's no way that's going to happen. Instead, I use the branches to pull myself downriver, looking for some spot to clamber out.

Forty yards down there's a place with something like a slope to it. There is no graceful way to do this. Using my left leg and my left arm, I hoist myself into the branches, onto the dirt. My boat bobs out from underneath me and my right half dunks into the frigid river. The smack of icy water pushes me to fight through the pain. With a scream I pull myself out of the water.

Clinging to the rhododendron, I turn to see my empty boat drift away into the foggy darkness. It looks like home, like safety and something good, and I'm sad to see it go. Surprisingly sad to see it go.

"Good-bye, little boat," I say. "Thank you."

It disappears into the night, gone from me forever.

The climb up to the road is brutal. I am climbing through as much as I am climbing up. Rhododendron and mountain laurel cover the steep hillside, creating an almost impenetrable thicket of rough-barked branches. Every ten feet I stop to breathe. The road is so far away, but at least it's there.

It's amazing that car drove by when it did. Otherwise I never would have known I'd sailed past what I spent so long searching for. What if it hadn't gone by at that moment? Where would I have found myself? Lost in a wilderness too thick to escape? Possibly. I must be thankful and know I'm in God's hands. That car feels like proof that providence will lead me to safety.

These good feelings of meant-to-be keep me going up the side of the embankment, keep me going all the way to the guardrail. I pause to touch the metal. It's like a blessing, although whether the guardrail is blessing me or I'm blessing it, I couldn't say. It's just important to mark this occasion. The road is before me. I've made it.

Five Years Ago

EVERYTHING IS PACKED UP AND READY TO GO. THE HORSE IS in the trailer, one last check to make sure taillights and blinkers work. The girl has opted to ride with the boy and his mother. Her grandmother is riding shotgun, so she climbs into the backseat of their station wagon, next to the boy. She is exhausted. So, so exhausted.

There is silence for a few minutes. All she wants is for that silence to go on forever, to go from Oklahoma to South Carolina.

The boy's mother decides to make conversation. "So, school is around the corner. Are you excited to go to the new middle school, Ruth?"

"Haven't thought about it." She uses the tone of voice that means stop talking, and the woman takes the hint.

The girl looks over at the boy, in his old Wranglers and stained white T-shirt. He is never going to change. He is going to be a social liability for the rest of their lives.

The boy turns to look at her, smiles. He's wearing the cross he's worn ever since his father left. She has spoken to him about the Wranglers, but she wouldn't dare address the cross. And it's not that she doesn't share his faith. She does. They are in their church youth group together. But the boy is the president of the youth group, and he isn't shy about that fact. He'll tell anybody all about it.

She doesn't mean to, but she sighs.

"You okay?" the boy asks.

"I'm just tired. Really, really tired."

CHAPTER NINETEEN

BECAUSE I CRAWLED UP THE FAR SIDE, I NEED TO CROSS the bridge. Although I don't believe the search-and-rescue people will find me, it would be stupid not to head their way. The helicopter, the sound of the dogs, all of that pulls me down the road. Not only that, but my best guess is that the town I saw from the mansion is in the same direction. It's hard to say, after getting lost, but my gut says the town, the search and rescue, all of it is on the other side of the bridge.

Walking across the bridge is eerie. The river is far below me, but the fog hides any clue of just how high up I am. If anything, the fog is even thicker up here. There's not a lot to see, but what can be seen looks old. The pavement is cracked; the guardrail is rusted. This isn't a big freeway with a bunch of lanes and fresh asphalt. It's an old two-lane country highway. But beggars can't be choosers. It's a road. It's paved. It's going somewhere, and at some point someone will drive past. I'm so close to saved I already know what it feels like.

Finding the road must have given me a boost of adrenaline. Or maybe it was optimism. Whatever it was, it's gone again. The parts of me that are wet have turned to ice. My feet hurt. My shoulders hurt. The only thing I have in all the world is the white line in front of me. I follow it like a drunk taking a field sobriety test.

I wish I had the moon to talk to. Of course, the moon still hangs in the sky, far beyond the fog, but that's not good enough. I need to see him to talk to him. At this point I'd settle for being able to see some trees, or even the far side of the road.

How long I walk before I hear an engine, I don't know. But it's like hearing angels sing. The car is far away, giving me a chance to prepare myself. I can't screw this up. I can't.

A new wrinkle presents itself. With this fog they won't see me until they're on top of me. I stand close to the yellow line. Walking on the shoulder of the road might say "I'm minding my own business." Standing in the middle of the road says "I'm in trouble." I slip off my coat, both because my white T-shirt underneath will show up better and so I can flag them down with the jacket.

All I can see are headlights in the mist. I start waving the jacket, just in case they already see me. I want to wave the jacket hard, above my head, but my damn arms won't do it. I have to settle for a strange matador-type motion.

The headlights are close now. This is it.

I flap the jacket harder, as hard as I can.

I edge as close to the yellow line as I dare.

Here it comes.

"Help!" I don't know if they can hear me, but I scream anyway. "Help!"

In less than a second the car takes shape out of the mist. It is new and black, with four doors. It swerves to avoid me even as it smacks me with the blare of its horn. It accelerates away, its red taillights looking angry in the night. Then it is gone. Altogether gone.

"Idiot!" I want to throw something at it. "You idiot! What do you think? You think I want to be here? You think this is fun? You think I'm crazy?" I pause. "Well, you'd be right on that last point." There is the tiniest bit of humor that comes out of saying that, but that glimpse of normalcy only makes everything worse. There is nothing normal here, nothing funny. Nothing good.

For a while there's nothing I can do but stand in the middle of the road, because going forward hurts too much. Going forward means continuing to try, when trying is so hard. The world is filled with idiots and assholes and monsters. Where are the guardian angels? Where are the decent people? Where are the people with sense? Where have they all disappeared to? Why try, when no one will help me? No one will ever help me. I am alone.

I return to my long walk to nowhere.

No. Not alone. My family and friends care. More than care. They love me. People are searching for me. I lost hold of these facts once, and I can't afford to do it again. It's important to hold on to this.

My family and friends love me. People are searching for me. These things are real. I cannot see them, but I must believe they're real.

I stick to the yellow line. Might as well stay in the center. It would take energy to move over to the side. The one good thing about the silence is that no cars are going to sneak up on me.

As I walk, I try to force myself to remember the faces of loved ones, envision rescue teams searching for me. It even occurs to me the idiot driver might call 911 to say there's a crazy person bothering cars out in the middle of nowhere. Or maybe they were shocked by the sight of me and only later realized I was in trouble.

So far the highway has sloped gently downhill. It didn't dawn on me that I should be grateful for that until the slope switches dramatically. Now, as I climb steadily uphill, everything becomes harder. No energy for positive thoughts. No energy for anything but putting one foot in front of the other.

The fog remains oppressive. My cold flesh is now numb. The hill will never end. One foot in front of the other. Every step dulls my senses until it feels as though the fog has taken over my brain along with the rest of the world.

With a blaze of light and the roar of an engine everything changes. I didn't know it, but I'm almost at the peak of the mountain. Cresting the hill is a giant SUV going fast. I'm on the yellow line and way too close for comfort. Instinct takes over and I jump out of the way. The speeding SUV hits the brakes as it passes me. I take off my jacket and start waving it. The SUV keeps going, but at a slower pace.

I run toward the car. "Stop! Stop!"

It's going to stop. I can tell it's going to stop. Everything's going to be okay.

But then the SUV picks up speed.

My run turns into a sprint, and I flap my jacket harder. "Stop! Please stop!"

The SUV pulls away from me and drives off into the night.

"Oh God." *Don't cry. Don't despair.* "Oh God, why?" *Stay positive. Stay positive.* "Why are you doing this to me?" *Think of the good things. That driver had doubts. I know that driver had doubts. They thought about stopping. They might be calling 911 right now.* "What did I do to deserve this?" *Stop crying. Now.* "I wasn't perfect; I know I wasn't; I know all the bad things I've done. But I don't deserve this. I don't." *Get a hold of yourself.*

Breathe.

I obey myself. I breathe. I breathe for a while.

Now think. Why isn't this working?

These idiots are scared of me. That's what it is. These idiots are scared. It baffles me how anybody could be scared of a teenage girl who probably weighs less than a hundred pounds at this point, but they are. I pause to consider myself.

I'm wearing a puffy camo trucker hat and a giant camo jacket. Underneath that is a filthy, man's white T-shirt. On my legs are oversize socks tied with laces, making them look like saggy makeshift Roman sandals. Around my waist is a holster and a handgun. Not sure if the gun works after getting dunked in the river, but it's there.

I need to change tactics.

Five Days Ago

IT IS FOUR IN THE MORNING WHEN THE MAN PARKS HIS truck behind a line of Bradford pears. The bushy trees, now a dusky autumnal red, shield the service entrance to the ranch from view, as well as his old truck. He believes she will arrive in an hour, but it's important to account for variables. Leaving his vehicle behind, he stations himself behind the two tractors. From here he can see his own truck, the main drive, and the entrance to the barn. It's perfect.

The weather has been up and down lately. It's chilly now, but the man wears a thick flannel shirt, woolen cap, and leather gloves. The leather gloves are dual purpose.

Time slips by in peaceful fashion, as it does whenever he is in the zone. He checks his watch. It's almost five.

Headlights come up the main drive.

She is punctual, he'll give her that. It is still dark as night, and there isn't a soul around. If he'd written a script, he couldn't have created a better scenario.

She disappears into the barn. The faint glow of the tack room light flicks on.

It's go time.

CHAPTER TWENTY

THE FOG HAS LIFTED SOME. THE SKY REMAINS STARLESS, but at least the trees are visible again. This is good. This is necessary. Necessary for my plan to work. It's not without risk, but I'm done hoping. It's time to force things to happen.

Time is never easy to measure alone in the wilderness, but it's not too long before the deep rumble of an engine tells me to get ready. My heart is in my throat as I lie down in the middle of the road, across the yellow line.

I cover up the gun with the flap of my jacket. I don't want to abandon it, but I don't want anybody to see it either. The trick is to not move a muscle, to appear unconscious. An unconscious body is not scary at all. It is helpless and in need of help. I'm determined to hold on to stillness as long as I can.

There's a chance the driver could be on their phone or dozing off or messing with the radio. There's a chance that I'll have to scramble for safety, and I'll run straight into the car. There's a chance I'll die. But I think there's a better chance that a girl lying in the middle of the road will get the help she needs.

Seconds stretch into forever. Will the car see me? Will they stop? They might swerve to avoid me, go up on the shoulder and continue on into the night. They could be like everybody else who has come before them.

The squeal and squeak of brakes tell me the car is slowing, then stopping. I turn to see my rescuer, but the headlights blind me. The driver's side door opens with a loud creak.

The headlights are big, round. High up off the ground. Funnily enough, it's the headlights that tell me what I've done. They're old-fashioned truck headlights, the kind you don't see very often anymore.

When his frame steps in front of the light, it's what I expect to see. The massive outline of Wolfman.

It's not that I don't try to get away, it's just that I don't succeed.

His giant fist grabs my holster belt. I remember the terror of his inexorable strength. He picks me up by my waist, snatches the gun, and tosses me into the cab in one smooth motion.

There are no words. Not from him. Not from me.

This isn't cute for him anymore. This is business now. This is death.

The gun is against my temple as he puts the truck into drive. Even though he has to reach across with his left hand to the gear shift, the movement doesn't look awkward. It looks deadly in its controlled power.

He steps on the gas, and we move off into the night. Wolfman doesn't want to shoot me inside his truck. Too messy. He wants to take me to the nearest side road and kill me there, in the woods. This is going to happen. I am going to die.

I am going to die.

These words rest inside my head in a new way. It's not like the whispering, insidious voice that said *Maybe you're meant to die out here.* This is different. This is real. It is not weakness and pain and self-pity. It is clarity and awareness and strength.

I am going to die. This is going to happen.

And it's okay.

I don't want to die, and I will not submit without a fight. But I am not afraid to die either. Because it's okay. It's okay. My life has been filled with countless mistakes, but also success. I have been a coward at some points, but brave at others. I have loved and been loved; I have failed to love and to accept love. Above all else I have tried my best, every step of the way. I tried to be good and did those things I thought were good to do. I fought hard to live a life worthy of the gift God gave me. What more could I have done? I could have done no more with what I had at the time.

I let go of the idea that the past could have been any different than it was.

If I should live, and I will do everything in my power to make that happen, my life will never be the same, and I will be better for it. But I am going to die. And that's okay. I have faith I will go to a better place.

All of this runs through my mind in less than a second. I have a plan, a way to fight before I go, but before I can put it into effect, something happens.

A cop drives by.

Both Wolfman and I see it. Having just put his truck in gear, he's driving at a suspiciously slow pace. That cop is no coincidence. The SUV did come through for me. The SUV called 911. That cop is looking for me. I'm certain of it, because my gut tells me so.

The wheels turn behind Wolfman's orange eyes. He's checking the rearview mirror more than he's looking at the road ahead of him. My plan is put on hold, waiting to see if the cop flips a U-turn and appears behind us. Wolfman watches the mirror, I watch Wolfman, and both of us wait to see what fate has in store.

The cop doesn't show.

Wolfman lets go of a long breath. That's my cue.

"I know you're going to kill me."

He says nothing, doesn't even look at me.

"I am going to die unpurified. Unrepentant. And without fear. Look at me."

He doesn't look.

"Look at me. Look me in the eyes."

Wolfman turns to see me, strangely obedient. Except it's not so strange. I can feel my own power. In a way it doesn't surprise me that he does what I tell him to do.

"I'm not scared of you. I'm not scared of death. You may kill me, but you're not going to beat me."

His eyes are as empty as ever, still far emptier than an animal's eyes, but it doesn't take heart or soul to realize I'm right.

Wolfman realizes I am right. I can see it in him. I can see the hate, the powerful, overwhelming hate. The devil himself could not look at me with more hate. I would be scared out of my wits, but there's nothing to be scared of now. I already know what's going to happen.

And that's when I bite his hand.

My arms are no good, but my jaw works. His hand becomes a fist that smashes my head into the seat, the window, the door. But I'm a pit bull that won't let go. Blood fills my mouth. Flesh tears in my teeth. My job is to fight as hard as I can, for as long as I can.

I hang on for a few seconds more. Wolfman rips his hand free, aims the gun at my face, and pulls the trigger.

Nothing happens.

The gun misfired. Whether it's two days in the grit and wet of the river or providence, I don't know, but it makes me fight even harder. Using teeth and nails I try to force the gun out of his fist. Wolfman needs both hands to clear the bullet from the chamber. He's strong enough to drag me over to the driver's side. My ribs hit the steering wheel, and I get a new idea.

Crash the truck.

Forcing my body between him and the windshield, I push my back into the steering wheel. It's the best I can do without letting go of the gun. The truck zigzags down the highway. Hope rises as it goes to two wheels, but then it slams back down to earth, jostling me out of position. I sail back to the passenger side.

It's the break Wolfman needed. With lightning speed he clears the jammed gun and points it back at my head. In the dim, green light emanating from the dashboard his hand shines with blood. I'm thinking he no longer cares if his truck gets messy.

Before he pulls the trigger, a brighter light, a white light, fills the cab of the truck. Headlights. From behind us. He lowers his gun hand to hide the weapon from view, jamming the muzzle up against my heart.

"Move one more time and I pull the trigger."

"Is it the cop?"

He says nothing.

"It is, isn't it? He's following us."

"One more time, I pull the trigger."

The question becomes whether or not Wolfman will make good on his threat. I think he's bluffing. If he shoots me, he'll likely be killed by the policeman. If not killed outright, then caught and killed on death row. Pulling the trigger right now would mean a terrible outcome for Wolfman.

Does he hate me enough to sentence himself to that future? I don't think so. He's still driving slowly. Slowly enough that I'm thinking I can jump out and survive. I've fallen off bolting horses, landed on rocky ground. Didn't even break a bone. Horses get close to forty miles per hour. I can't see the speedometer, but it feels slow.

I might not make it, but this police car is a chance I can't waste.

Breathing deep, I count down in my head. *Three, two, one.* On one I unlock the passenger-side door. Rip open the handle. Slam my body into door. Sail out into the night.

Somewhere in there came a gunshot, deafeningly loud in the confines of the cab. Somewhere in there came a massive impact. Whether it was a bullet or hitting pavement, I don't know. Somewhere in there was gravel and my spinning body and pain.

Sound happens first. Scrape. Scrape. Scrape. It scratches at the surface of my brain until I open my eyes. The truck looms over me. The edge of the police cruiser is visible behind it. The vehicles are dark and silent. The scraping is coming from somewhere else.

Rolling my head over, I see the source of the sound. Two feet. It's so dark and foggy it's hard to tell what I'm looking at. Eventually I realize those feet are being dragged. The heels are scraping along the road.

It's the policeman. He's dead.

Wolfman has him under the armpits. He's pulling him off into the forest.

I have no room for emotion, but the thought floats through my mind that this man is dead because of me. I jumped because he was behind me. I jumped because I thought he could save me. But there is no saving anyone from Wolfman.

Turning the other way, I discover the guardrail above me. This is the edge of the road. Wolfman needs to dispose of the body and hide the car. Maybe he won't notice I'm gone. Getting up is an impossibility; I don't even try it. Instead, I squirm and push and kick my way through the posts. Below me is a grass-covered hill. I begin to slither my way down. Everything is broken now. Ribs are definitely broken. My legs are raw from road rash. It's nothing but pain, so I leave my body. Floating above myself, I watch as I work my way down the hillside.

It's fog and darkness and rocky ground. It's belly-to-the-dirt army crawl. It's the only thing I can do. My right shoulder is almost useless, making me veer in that direction.

I reach the bottom of the hill and enter a flat field. The grass is high. The fog is thick. The wilderness is silent. The world becomes small, just the foot of space before me, beside me, behind me. It's good that the world has become so small. It makes it easier to do my work. To keep moving.

Grandpapa walks toward me, his hands cupped. We had a picnic outside tonight. Ribs, potato salad, sweet tea. We feasted on summer and it tasted so good. Now I'm chasing lightning bugs in the dusk, but they stay three steps ahead of me.

"Ruthie, come here," he says, his voice even lower and slower than usual.

I trot over to him, rise up on tiptoes, try to see what's in his hands. He squats down, but his hands are held together, a hollow ball with something inside.

"Be very quiet."

I do as I'm told, holding my breath, waiting for the moment of discovery. What does Grandpapa have? It must be something glorious.

With great care, Grandpapa opens his hands. On his palm sits a beetle. There's a patch of red behind its head, orange outlines its long, slender body, but these colors are not bright or special. Mostly it's a plain little insect.

I open my mouth to speak, but Grandpapa says, "Shhh . . ."

So I keep staring at the beetle.

Then it glows, a yellow-green living miracle.

I'm not moving anymore. That's not good. I went away for a while, and when I came back, I wasn't moving anymore. It comes to me that Grandpapa would want me to move. He'd want me to keep going.

Getting going hurts. It hurts so much I sail up out of my body again and watch it work from a safe distance. From up here it's interesting, more than anything else. It's strange how I move. Like a spider that's missing some legs. I've never liked killing anything, but I've put spiders like that out of their misery. A quick stomp and then no more herky-jerky movement, just a smear on the ground.

I don't want to be put out of my misery, though. I want to live. I want to go back to good things.

The sun is getting too close to the horizon. Once it disappears completely, I've got to go in for dinner, which means there's not enough time to finish our fort today. It's the best fort Caleb and I have ever made. It goes out into the river, so there's an on-land section of it and an indoor-pool section of it.

"Hand me that twine," Caleb says.

I give him the rope while I shovel wet gravel. I'm bolstering the main wall of the indoor swimming pool.

"When we grow up we should make a house for real just like this," I say. "Have it go out over the river. There'd be glass floors and you could look down and see the water."

"What if it floods?" Caleb is always practical.

"You'd put it up on stilts like houses at the beach, so if it floods it just hits the stilts."

"That'd be cool. And it could be really tall, too, up into the branches of the trees, like a tree house."

I like it when Caleb plays along. "And instead of beds we'd have hammocks," I say.

"And you could make me dinner every night."

I laugh long and hard. "In your dreams." Upon reflection, I add, "I would make breakfast, though, because I like doing it. You can make dinner."

"Deal."

A thud wakes me up. Somehow I know the thud was me falling to the ground. Which means I must have been up and walking. There's no memory of being up and walking, but I'm sure that's what was going on.

Scattered pine trees surround me. Where did the flat field go? I have no idea. All I know is that I was visiting the memory of a long-gone fort. I'd completely forgotten that ever happened. The next day we discovered the river had washed away all our hard work. Why didn't we rebuild? Even now, nine years later, I think that fort was pretty amazing.

Wait, no. This isn't important. I shouldn't be thinking about a fort. There are pine needles stuck to my face. I'm facedown in a pine forest. I need to be thinking about how to survive.

I was walking and that's good. I know that's good. I need to see if I can do it again.

Getting up is an otherworldly torture. Once up I decide to never fall down ever again. Doing that twice would be too much to ask of my body. Moving forward is a lot to ask too. That feeling of leaving myself comes over me again. I don't think it's a good thing. Fighting the sensation, I try to stay in the pain, stay with my legs and my arms, my head and my stomach. I try to remember the Wolfman.

Up ahead there's a patch of forest that seems brighter than the rest. It doesn't look like the dawn, although the sun can't be too far off. It doesn't look like much of anything at all, actually. It might not even really be there. But it gives me something to focus on, something to dull the pain. I wonder if the glow is emanating from the redheaded girls. I don't see them, but that doesn't mean they're not there. They haven't steered me wrong yet, so I point my feet in their direction.

After a few more yards I decide that the light is real. It's not the other girls. It's too big and bright for that. It's a bluish-white sort of color. There's something very pure about it. In the mist it dissipates into a broad, soft glow. No sign to be seen of what is behind it. It almost makes me think of heaven. It's possible I could be walking toward heaven. I have no idea what it's like. My pastor said that before you went to heaven, you were baptized by a Pentecostal fire. It wasn't clear what he meant by that, but it stuck with me. Maybe this pain is a Pentecostal fire. Maybe I'm getting ready to go to heaven. Maybe that white light will be the end of all of this. I don't want it to be the end, but if that's what God has planned for me, it'll be okay.

My mom is in the doorway, a cardboard box labeled GOODWILL under one arm and a DVD in her hand. She looks concerned, or maybe just a little sad.

"You're giving away *The Black Stallion*?"

"Yeah."

"I thought maybe it got in here on accident, or something."

"Nope."

"I thought it was your favorite movie."

I shrug.

"Not anymore?"

"I'm never going to watch it again, Mom." This is a true statement.

"Too old for it now, I guess."

"I guess." But my agreement is a lie. It's not that I'm too old for it. It's that I know the end will make me cry, and I can't have that. A new trailer-load of training horses arrived today. The business is taking off, Regionals are next week, and I need to win to keep the clients coming. At our last youth group meeting we read the part of Corinthians where it talks about putting away childish things. I'm thirteen. It's time for the childish things to go away. It's time to stop believing in fairy tales.

◆ ◆ ◆

I've managed to prop myself up against a tree. How long I've been resting against it, I have no idea. I'm proud of myself though. I promised to never fall down again, and I managed to avoid that by resting against this tree. Even so, it's worrying that the drifting-away thing happened again. It's getting so hard to stay. There's something important, though. Something I need to remember.

My head lolls back against my will.

"No. Wake up." Snapping back upright, I say, "What is it?"

Inside, I answer, *I don't know.*

But there was something. There was definitely something.

The light. I'm walking toward a light. It's not ahead of me anymore. It's strange, though. Everything seems a little lighter. The mist diffuses the light, so it's not easy to say if this is morning or what. Looking around, I find the bright light to my left. Striking off toward it, I decide it's brighter than before, but not by much. During my drifting off I think I veered away from the light. Hard to say. I was visiting another memory from the far-distant past.

I won my first Worlds title five years ago. Feels like a thousand lifetimes. Feels like I've been Ruth Carver, show beast from hell, my whole life, that there was never a time before it. But there was a time. A little window of time where I caught fireflies and built forts and watched *The Black Stallion.* Why did I stop all that? Why did I turn off all the switches inside? Was that necessary?

I have no idea. All I know is, I put myself into a box. In that box I could have Becca and Courtney, but them not even very much, and Caleb, in the weird way I had Caleb. That was my box. That's what I got. Everything else was for the greater glory of the

Carver name. But there wasn't much joy in it. It was a mission to be accomplished.

As much as I love my mother, as much as I want to hug her and tell her how much I've missed her, as I think about my box and how little was inside it, resentment flares up within me. I've carried an awful lot for a long, long time. More than a teenage girl should.

I've carried an awful lot these last few days. More than anyone ever should.

But the light is there. It is real. I'm walking toward it, and the world is a lighter shade of gray than it was before. I have no idea how I'm walking at all. I can only think that I'm not the one responsible, that God is guiding me to the place I'm supposed to go.

Something flashes to my right, a moving strobe light through the trees. In a second it is gone, but I realize what it was. A car driving down a road on the other side of the forest. I pause for a second, debating. Should I veer toward the road or keep going toward the light? Pain insists I pick quickly, and I stay on the path toward the light. The road isn't safe, and Wolfman is out there.

The thought of him sparks a new energy. I'm able to stay in the pain and in my body without drifting away. I'm able to focus on what's ahead. It's some sort of man-made light. A cluster of them, high up off the ground.

Fighting the drift away, I stare at the ground, picking my way with care, trying to make things easier on my broken body. When I look up again, I recognize what I'm walking toward. It's a gas station. A great big, newly built gas station. It's probably two football fields away.

Another set of headlights strobes its way through the trees. The road must lead to the gas station. The road is closer to me than it was before. Much closer. I don't like that. I don't want to be near roads anymore.

The headlights turn around, blinding me for a second. I watch as they bounce up and down as the truck pulls over to the side of the road. The truck goes dark as the driver turns off the headlights, but I can make out the shape of the truck as it heads into the trees.

I can think of only one reason why someone driving a truck, upon spotting me, would turn off their headlights and go off-roading in my direction.

I attempt to run. It isn't a run. It's a broken shuffle. But I broken shuffle as best I can. I glance back once. The truck is parked. He's pulling some kind of long stick thing out of the bed. After that, no more glancing back. Just broken shuffling and pulling in a giant lungful of air so I can yell "Help!"

It doesn't sound like much.

I keep trying.

He's closing the gap. Not with a broken shuffle but with a dead run.

There's no way I can get to the gas station before he gets me. The best thing I can do is yell "Help" as many times as I can, as loud as I can, while shuffling forward.

I think it's five times before the train slams into my back, sending me breathless to the dirt.

Rolling over, I see him standing over me. That long stick thing was a shovel. He has the gun, too, but I can sense what's about to happen before it happens. He's going to throttle me to death. It's quieter that way. He wants this to be quiet.

There's so little left in me, but what little there is wants to struggle, hit, maim, bite, kick, hurt. I want to win. So desperately, I want to win. I want to win my way, but I can't. My body is done.

There is only one thing left for me to do.

Pretend to die.

I lie motionless as he straddles my stomach. Not fighting back is the hardest thing I've ever done, but he won't quit until I'm dead and so dead I must be. I will win with strategy, not strength. The true victory is escaping with my life, and a win is a win, even an ugly one. And this is ugly. His body pushes into mine, cutting into my breath, crushing my stomach, making all of my hurt hurt even more.

Wolfman pauses, looking off into the distance. Maybe he's hearing something I'm not, or maybe he wants to be sure my calls for help go unanswered. Satisfied, he turns his gaze back to me. His eyes are obscured by the darkness, but the searing heat of hate radiates out of them all the same. If anything, it's grown since I felt it in the cab of the truck. Energy burns through his body and into mine, electric with the need to not just kill me, but destroy me. My flesh comes alive with the frantic need to escape and it takes every bit of willpower I have to resist, to lie there, to pretend that I have no strength left at all.

He bends down until we are nose to nose. The smell of him, of his stale breath, nauseates me. Still I lie there, unmoving. He grabs my jaw in his massive hand, squeezing it, forcing it open. Then he puts his tongue into my mouth. By no definition is this a kiss. This is suffocation—forcible, horrific suffocation. I try and try and try not to fight, but instinct takes over and I squirm and struggle to get away, to get air.

"Hey! Is anybody out there?"

Somebody from the gas station. It's a man. He sounds young. Wolfman sits up, his head swiveling toward the lights. The fog has lifted some, and I wonder how much the man can see.

"Anybody?"

I suck in cold, clean air with everything I have. Instinct tells me to shout for help, but then Wolfman puts his hand on his gun.

"Did somebody call for help out here?"

The cop is dead because I thought he could save me. I've heard only a handful of words out of this man from the gas station, but he means the world to me. He's a stranger who wants to help another stranger. He's not like the Logans or the people who drove past me on the highway. He's good, and he's trying to help. He has no idea, but he already has helped, just by wanting to. No matter what, I have to protect him.

Minutes pass in silence. The gas station man must have given up.

Wolfman turns back to me. His body tenses, like he's made a decision and is steeling himself. Letting go of his gun, he grabs hold of my throat.

This is it. I can't break again. I can't give in to the panic.

He squeezes and I thrash around, careful to appear feeble, but not so feeble as to be unbelievable. I also try to stay quiet; I don't want the gas station man to hear and come running. Wolfman bears down. My air is going. Quickly. Too quickly. I can't pass out. If I'm unconscious, I'll lose control and die.

I lock my gaze on the sky above me, praying to God for strength.

The clouds part and the moon, my friend the moon, shines hazily above me, ringed in a halo.

It is my cue. I let my body fall limp.

Wolfman doesn't stop squeezing.

Hello, Moon, I think. *I'm glad I got to see you again. I might be joining you soon.*

No, says Moon, *not yet.*

Wolfman releases my throat.

I stare, glassy-eyed, at the moon, holding my breath to almost nothing.

Wolfman picks up the shovel and goes to work. While he digs, I practice. There's a strange feeling of relaxing into it, of being at peace with my eyes wide open, my breath a barely there open-mouthed hiss. Moon said *not yet* and I believe him. I find the power in playing dead.

I play dead for what feels like an eternity while Wolfman digs.

In the distance a siren wails.

The digging stops. One arm and a leg of mine are grabbed, but I don't feel it much. Like a method actor, I'm too dead to feel what the living would. My body slides across the dirt and slumps into a shallow pit. The moon still glows above me, and my open eyes still see him. My view of the moon is interrupted by the shape of Wolfman, busily scraping and dumping and pushing dirt onto me.

Help me, Moon. It's coming.

I'm here. I've always been here. Even when you couldn't see me.

A mix of dirt and leaves and pine needles covers my neck. Now my mouth. I push my tongue forward to protect my throat. Over my nose now, the filth comes. It's about to cover my eyes.

The siren grows louder.

I don't blink. I don't breathe. I am dead. I am dead, I am dead, I am dead.

Courage, says Moon.

I feel it hit my eyeballs, but still I do not blink.

It covers my ears, and sound goes away.

Blackness now and nothing more. But I know the moon is there, even if I can't see him.

Slowly, carefully, I close my eyes, letting my tears wash away the grit. Slowly, carefully, I use my tongue to create a pocket around my mouth so I can breathe. There isn't much air, but there is some.

My resolution is to wait as long as I possibly can. I am dead.

Sirens again. Loud enough I can hear them inside my tomb. It's time, but I don't know where to start. Nothing wants to move. I ask my arms first, then my legs. No response.

Come on! I yell at them. *Move!*

My body has gotten too good at playing dead.

Kick! I tell my legs. *Kick hard!*

My left leg moves. Then my right. Things are starting to happen. Even my arms, but them only a little bit. I try to sit up.

Something grabs my leg. It's a hand. The terror of being touched pushes me to fight harder. My hand punches through and it's grabbed too, and now I'm being touched all over. There are voices, but they're distant, like a radio stuck between channels. I struggle against the voices and hands.

One moment I am underground and the next moment I'm above it. I can barely see, everything is bleary and painful with dirt. It's not night anymore, but it isn't really morning yet either. Two cops are kneeling on either side of me. I think of the other cop, the dead cop, probably a friend of theirs, and I know I have to warn them.

"He's out there!" The words come out garbled. I spit out some leaves and dirt and try again. "His name is Jerry T. Balls."

"Ruth, we know. We know who you are. We have you."

"He killed a cop. He's out there. His truck was right by those trees over there."

"Please try to relax for us, Ruth."

"His name is Jerry T. Balls."

One of the cops stands and begins talking into his radio. I can't quite make out what he's saying. Everything is confused, a blur I can't quite get straight.

Then a new face enters my view, a different sort of face. It's a man. About twenty. He has scruffy facial hair, and he's wearing a uniform with a patch name tag that says *Sean* in cursive.

"Is this her?" he asks. Nobody answers the obvious question. Sean's eyes go to mine. "I'm so sorry I didn't go out into the woods. I was pretty sure I heard somebody yelling for help."

I shake my head as tears flood my eyes and emotion closes my throat.

"I'm so, so sorry."

"He would have killed you," I say, but it comes out in choking sobs. I don't think he understood me. Whether he can make out my words or not, he seems to understand my expression, because he reaches out and grabs my arm.

"Oh man, I'm just so sorry."

The kneeling cop says, "Hey, you called 911. You saved her."

I reach out and put my hand over Sean's. I try very hard to be clear. "Thank you."

He doesn't say anything. I think he may be crying. But he squeezes my hand. I focus in on that pressure and close my eyes.

"Keep doing that," the cop says to Sean. "It's helping."

I open my eyes to what seems like a hundred people in fluorescent vests hovering over me. Above and beyond them, morning has taken hold. A golden light fills the mist, creating a soft glow over everything. It's strange, though, because the light isn't just gold—other colors dance through the fog. Blue and red and a deeper amber. It's subtle, though, so much so that I'm not sure if it's real.

I'm still on the ground. Someone is holding my hand—it's Sean. He hasn't left me, and I give him a squeeze of thanks, which he returns, but a swarm of EMTs are taking over. "Sir," one of them says. "You're going to need to step aside, sir."

Sean fades away, now outside my field of vision. There's a momentary feeling of panic when he leaves, but it's overwhelmed by hands and equipment and voices and sounds, until I'm not feeling anything at all. It's like I'm still underground, still dead within my tomb.

The EMTs say soothing things, but I don't listen or care. I can see their faces, but they mean nothing to me. People put an oxygen mask over my mouth, but I don't care about that, either. They come along with a board and put me on it, put my neck into a brace. That's okay. But then they try to strap me down and a new panic takes over. The ropes take me right back to Wolfman and I see him before me. I see him so clearly I think he's really there.

"No ropes! Don't tie me up!"

"It's okay," an EMT says. "These are straps, not ropes. They're for your safety."

"No ropes!"

I squeeze my eyes shut as I struggle. One EMT, a woman, leans in and speaks into my ear. Her voice is low and matter-of-fact. "I need you to breathe for me, Ruth. Breathe in deep, breathe out slowly."

At first I can't do it, but I can key in to her voice. She sounds confident, there's a natural authority to her, and she repeats her instructions until I obey. I breathe until I stop struggling.

"We have to strap you in now. If you struggle, we will do it anyway." She isn't unkind, she's just letting me know how it is. I appreciate that. She reminds me of a horse trainer. I open my eyes. There are no more hallucinations of Wolfman. Instead, I focus on the calm EMT. She in her forties with dyed blond hair. She looks like she's lived a hard life, like she's seen things most people never do. It makes me trust her.

I still don't like those straps, but I stay quiet. They're like yellow seat belts, and they force me to the board and keep me there. Despite my efforts to breathe in deep and slowly, the panic creeps in around the edges. The woman can see I'm barely holding it together.

"What if we raise the upper portion so it's like you're sitting up? You want to try that?" Behind her, other EMTs protest, but she sticks a hand out, overruling their concerns with a gesture.

I lock onto her gaze and nod.

With a *crick,* the stretcher is popped up like a lawn chair and my whole world changes. I can see what's around me and I'm overcome in a whole new way. I've never seen so many emergency vehicles in all my life. The dancing lights in the mist are explained. Red and blue lights on cop cars, red lights on fire engines, amber lights on search-and-rescue vehicles—lights swirl everywhere around me. Where there aren't emergency vehicles or dark green DNR trucks, there are regular cars, and filling in the spaces in between are people. Dozens and dozens of people.

Most of them wear cheap fluorescent vests. It takes me a second, but I realize these are volunteers, people who have been searching for me in these mountains. In the early sunlight it isn't easy to see their faces, not from this far away, but I search the crowd and see no one I know. These are strangers who have been trying to find me.

Even if I can't see them well, I can feel their anxiety. Their energy is like a wave reaching out to me: their concern, their fear. Only then do I see the police tape that has been strung everywhere like holiday streamers. Cops and EMTs are on this side of the flimsy wall, the searchers on the other.

It strikes me—they don't know if I'm alive or dead.

So far I haven't felt much in the way of pain. Then they hoist the stretcher from the ground up to rolling height. The sudden jerk sets my body screaming. The blond EMT must have seen my expression because she's right back beside me.

"Keep breathing, Ruth. Focus on that for me. Breathe in, breathe out."

It's good having a job, it centers me, but it all feels so precarious.

We start our journey toward the ambulance. It's as if the stretcher has no shocks at all. The ground is smooth for a forest floor, but against my injuries it feels like a rumble strip. My whole world is breathing.

After a few feet a cop comes up alongside me and says, "Your family is already on the way to the hospital. They'll meet you there."

I see them in my mind, waiting for me. I see them overwhelmed and crying, and I recoil from the thought of it. I can't make this okay for them. I can't make it okay for me, let alone them.

My EMT looks concerned. "Don't worry about anything but breathing, okay?"

I nod, but that nod is a lie. Instead of focusing on my breathing, I remember imagining what it would be like walking out of the woods a triumphant hero. I imagined what it would be like, to cry and hold my family, my heart bursting with relief and joy. I never imagined that this moment would be nothing. I never imagined some stranger named Sean would spark more emotion in me than my own family.

My stretcher keeps rolling. It's a surreal method of locomotion. I search the yellow sky for the moon, missing him. He's not there. I need the moon. He'd understand me right now. Nobody else can understand me.

Finally, we reach pavement and my ride evens out. Now I can

see the crowd, all the volunteers. Each one is a stranger to me. Then I notice a man without a search-and-rescue vest. Taking him in, his expression, his energy, he feels different from the people with the vests on. It hits me that he is nothing but an onlooker, some guy who saw a commotion and wondered if he'd get to see a dead body or some blood.

Scanning the people pressed up against the police tape, I see more and more locals. There is a ghoulishness about their expressions that sickens me. My emptiness gives way to rage. I want to kill these onlookers. I can't kill them, so instead I stare at them, wanting to tell them with my eyes what I think of them. And there, tall enough to be seen in the back row, is Wolfman.

I gasp as if punched in the gut, but I don't believe my eyes. I've already hallucinated him once. The EMT stops the stretcher, thinking my reaction has something to do with my injuries.

Wolfman sees me, propped up and alive, and even from this distance I can see his surprise turn to hate. My reaction mirrors his because I know him. God knows, at this point I know him as I know myself, and I believe nothing more than that he'd come back to watch, supervise, get off on seeing my dead body carried away.

I scream.

Not in English, but in hate.

I twist my body into a pretzel, possessed. Writhing, twisting, I fight against all that binds me. The thin elastic band of my oxygen mask snaps. Broken as I am, I still want to kill him.

My EMT tries to replace it. I lock my gaze onto hers. I tell her, clearly and distinctly, "The man who took me is in the crowd."

I look back to where he was, and he's already gone. My scream wasn't smart. I let my hate get the best of me and gave him a chance to escape. I must be smart in how I speak. I must make these people believe.

"What?"

"The man who tried to kill me is in the crowd."

"Are you sure?"

I hear the power in my own voice as I tell her what she needs to know. "He is tall. Over six feet. He has dark hair and a beard. He was in the crowd, but he left as soon as he heard me scream."

I'm not sure what all is happening beyond the border of my stretcher, but cops and firemen appear. I keep talking, keep saying my message, like a general instructing soldiers going into battle. "The man who took me was in the crowd. He is over six feet tall. He has dark hair and a beard. He drives an old red pickup truck. He is middle aged." I say it again and again. People come and go, but I don't stop talking, don't stop repeating my message.

It feels like far too much time has gone by, but I don't stop giving instructions. It's the only thing I can do.

My EMT returns, puts her face close to my mine. "We have him. You can stop. We have him."

I hear her words, but I can't absorb them. "The man who took me is in the crowd."

"No, he's not. He's in a police car. We have him."

"You have him?" I don't sound like a general anymore. I sound broken.

"Yes, Ruth, we have him."

I believe her, but I can't stop talking now that I've started. "He killed a cop."

"Try to relax, okay?"

"He killed six girls."

"Please try to lie back and breathe."

"He killed six girls and he buried them under his cabin."

"Just lie back, okay?"

"He tried to kill me."

The EMT puts a new oxygen mask up to my face.

"He took me to a cabin in the woods and he was going to rape me, but I ran away."

"Let me put this on you."

"I ran away and I got to some people's house and they wouldn't help me. Why wouldn't they help me?"

"Calm down, Ruth. I need you to calm down."

"And then I took him. I took him hostage."

The EMT stops trying to put the mask on me. I know there are other people around, but I don't care, I'm just talking to this one woman, the woman with the calm, confident voice. I need this one person to understand.

"What?"

"I took him hostage, the man who kidnapped me. I tied him up. I did bad things. I tried to kill him with his own gun, but he got away and came back to get me again." I can't tell if she believes me or not.

"But then you got away, and now we've got him. You understand that, Ruth? You're safe."

I don't really think I'm safe, but I nod anyway and let her put the oxygen mask on me. The stretcher rattles along toward the ambulance. With a quick heave I'm up and in. Inside the ambulance I find a small dark cave. The lights glow dim. There's something soothing about this dark little cave. I keep my gaze on the blond EMT, the one who listened.

"What's your name?" I ask. She lifts up the mask and I repeat the question.

"Janet," she says. "I'm Janet. And I'm real proud of you, Ruth. I'm real proud of you."

The words mean a lot. Some of my clenched muscles let go.

"Would you do me one favor?" asks Janet. "Would you close your eyes?"

I do.

"Would you breathe real deep?"

I take a long, deep breath. More muscles unclench.

"Would you believe me when I tell you it's going to be okay?"

I don't believe her, but I nod anyway.

She pats my hand. "Good girl."

I know I'm in the hospital as soon as I wake up. It's night. There's a soft pool of light under the door; medical equipment buttons glow amber, red, and green. I turn my head, trying to get a sense of the space in the darkness. When I move, someone stands up. I'm not alone.

The weight of that knowledge, that someone is here, presses into me. I don't know much, but I know I don't want to talk to anyone. Don't want to explain anything. Don't want to hear someone cry over me. I want to be left alone.

From his silhouette I can tell it's Caleb.

That's something. I'd rather it be Caleb than anyone else.

"Ruth?"

"Yes?"

"You're awake." He pauses, as though waiting for me to speak. I don't. "Your parents are eating dinner in the cafeteria. I'll go get them."

"No." Only I don't just say no, I try to raise my arm, and the pain hits hard. I gasp and Caleb presses up against the bed and grabs my hand.

He whispers, "I'm so sorry, Ruthie."

But I don't want his pity. I turn away from him, as much as I am able.

"Ruth?"

"What?" I don't want to sound angry, but I know I do.

"Look at me." He says it with a firm authority that surprises me, so much so that I obey, trying to see his expression in the low light. There's no pity in him, only a fierce certainty.

"I love you, Ruth. You know that. Because I love you, I'm going to tell you the truth. And you're going to listen."

I do. I listen with everything I have.

"You're the strongest person I know. I've no idea what all you've gone through, but I bet most people wouldn't have made it, let alone gotten the one who did it. I heard the cops talking about you, and they couldn't believe what you did, spotting him in the crowd like that. You're a hero, Ruth."

I don't know what I wanted him to say, but it isn't this. I won,

I got the victory, I should be happy to know I succeeded, that no one else will suffer because of Wolfman, but instead the praise is suffocating.

Caleb's tone shifts, becoming stern. "Now, I know you won't want to hear this, but you've been too tough for your own good. For a long, long time now."

My heart skitters forward a few beats, and without thinking, I flip my hand around and grab Caleb. He's no longer holding on to me, I'm holding on to him.

"Believe me when I tell you—the strongest thing you can do right now is admit you're not strong enough to do this on your own."

I squeeze Caleb's hand. So hard it's like a death grip. He's right, I know he's right, but I have no idea how to do anything but be who I've always been. Caleb must think he hasn't gotten through, because he keeps preaching.

"You were strong enough to hold the farm together, you were strong enough to survive"—he pauses, not sure how to describe it—"everything you've survived, but you're not strong enough to do recovery alone. Nobody is."

It's so dark in the room I'm not sure if Caleb can tell I'm nodding. I'm nodding because I know if I speak I'll cry. I don't want to cry.

Caleb's voice is soft now, hushed. "It's okay to cry, Ruthie."

I fight it as hard as I can, but it's winning. My breathing spasms with the sobs I'm holding back.

"You are safe."

Without thinking, I say, "I don't think I am." I sound like an animal, the words mangled by emotion, but they're my truth. Caleb holds tight to my hand. I can feel his patience, his willingness to be a still center in the middle of my chaos. He is listening with all his might. There's no editor, no filter when I tell him, "I don't know how to be." I say it because I don't. I don't know how to be in this world, as this person. I don't know how to let people help me. I don't know how to let somebody else be in charge. I don't know how not to fight. Except, in a way, I do.

The sobs that were threatening to take over disappear. I take a deep breath. Caleb can feel the change, and he leans in, ready to hear what I have to say.

"At the end, he buried me. In the dirt. I couldn't fight anymore because everything was broken. I knew that to live, I had to play dead."

"That was smart, Ruthie. Real, real smart."

To my surprise, a spark of me comes alive, and I feel proud of myself. I say, "I kept my eyes open, even as the dirt hit."

Caleb doesn't say anything for a moment and the energy shifts. There's resistance, hesitancy in him. I can tell it's painful for him to learn these things, but he knows he has to hear that detail the way I want it to be heard. He has to be strong for me.

"Damn, girl . . . that psychopath picked the wrong target this time, didn't he?"

I laugh, and it feels like a miracle, because it means I'm still alive. I'm still alive inside this body. Wolfman didn't kill what makes me me. But he's also changed me forever. I'm overwhelmed with relief that a part of me lives on, and I'm overwhelmed with sadness that I'm broken, permanently damaged. My laugh melts into sobs. Caleb must think I've gone crazy.

He smooths back my hair. I can feel grit against my scalp. The dirt from my grave is still with me. The gentle touch calms me down some.

"Caleb, I want you to know that I know you're right. I know I'm not strong enough to do this on my own."

He exhales, tension leaving his body. "I'm so glad to hear you say that."

"I'm never going to be the same."

"No, you won't."

I shut my eyes and tears fall, but I appreciate his honesty.

"You're going to be better."

In shock, I look up at Caleb.

"It'll be a long, hard road, I don't deny that. But you can be better than you were before. I believe in you. You can do this. Everyone who loves you will be there every step of the way."

It is a stunning thought, a thought that feels like sunlight. I made it out. I have another shot at life. And that life could be anything.

"I should get your parents. They want to talk to you so bad."

A twinge of anxiety hits, but I nod.

"Thank you, Caleb."

He bends down and kisses me on the forehead. "I love you, Ruth."

"I love you, too. I'm so sorry I never said it before."

Caleb gives my hand one last squeeze and leaves the room. I hear him break into a jog once he's in the hallway. In the soft, safe peace of that dark hospital room, I am filled with gratitude that I've had the chance to tell Caleb I love him, that I have the chance to be better. There is hope for me.

Acknowledgments

Ben LeRoy, editor and professional awesome person, read this book when it was barely a book. He gave me the most useful notes I've ever received.

Debbie Vaughn, my cheerleader and coffee club buddy, believed in it from the start. Her enthusiasm meant the world and kept me going.

Danielle Stinson, who is a brilliant writer and a woman of strength and integrity, read it halfway through revisions. Her optimism gave me hope.

Tom Emmons, stand-up comedian and all-around creative genius, read it when I didn't know whether it was done or not. His confidence gave me the courage to send it out into the world.

Mandy Hubbard, who embodies the Platonic ideal of the literary agent, embraced this book wholeheartedly. She gave me the experience I'd been working toward for fourteen years.

Simon Pulse is the best home a writer could hope for. From Annette Pollert, who bought this book, to Patrick Price, who took it under his wing, to Michael Strother, who made it his own, the entire team has been amazing.

Fred and Irene Adams taught me to follow my bliss when I was a child. It is the greatest gift they could have given me, and their faith in my ability has been my fuel. I am so fortunate to have them for my parents.

This book would not have been possible without Evan Flower.